THE MOST DANGEROUS GAME

The Cyber asked, "Do you know the Quillian Sector?"

The hunter answered, "Parts well, other parts not so well, a little not at all. But then no one knows them. The worlds hidden in the cosmic dust and those caught in the mesh of destructive energies . . ."

"Yet you are confident that you can track Dumarest down in such a star cluster?"

"Guide me to a world and if he is on it, I will find him. More, give me cluster of worlds and I will show you which he will make for."

"Tell me one thing—aside from the reward, why do you want to hunt Dumarest?"

"Why?" Bochner inhaled, his breath a sibilant hiss over his teeth. "Because if half of what you've told me is true, then he is the most wily, the most dangerous and the most interesting quarry I could ever hope to find."

Also in Arrow by E. C. Tubb:

THE DUMAREST SAGA

THE QUILLIAN SECTOR

E. C. Tubb

ARROW BOOKS

Arrow Books Limited
17–21 Conway Street, London W1P 6JD

An imprint of the Hutchinson Publishing Group

London Melbourne Sydney Auckland
Johannesburg and agencies
throughout the world

First published in Great Britain 1982
© E. C. Tubb 1978

To Julie Emma Hickmott

Made and printed in Great Britain
by The Anchor Press Ltd
Tiptree, Essex

ISBN 0 09 929050 2

Chapter One

A great bowl of flowers had been set on a small table close to the window so that their petals reflected the light in a mass of glowing scarlet flecked with amber, the stamens a brilliant yellow around styles of dusty black. The bowl itself was of veined porphyry, shaped with a rare elegance, curves melting one into the other to form an object of both visual and tactile beauty. A thing of delicate elegance in direct contrast to the room itself, which was bleak in its Spartan simplicity, all white and functional, the walls devoid of any decoration, even the carpet a neutral gray.

A room in which to work, to study and to plan with all distraction kept to a minimum. Something Irae could appreciate, as he could not the flowers. They were an anomaly and he crossed the room to stand before them, studying their form and arrangement before lifting his head to stare through the window itself.

It was set high in the building and framed a view of grim desolation. The soil had been leached to expose the underlying rock, the vegetation which once had covered it long since gone, as were the minerals once contained within the stone. Machines had dug and ripped and crushed and spewed their detritus, turning a pleasant landscape into a barren wilderness. Exploitation had left nothing but sourness and acid rains which, even as he watched, came to add more corrosion to the thick pane and the metal in which it was set.

Looking down, he could now understand the presence of the flowers; the contrast they provided to the desolation outside.

"Caradoc's work," said a voice behind him. "He said that a touch of color would help."

5

Turning, Irae said, "Help whom? You?"

An accusation, which Yoka dismissed with a small gesture of a hand which seemed to be fashioned from transparent porcelain. No cyber was ever fat, for excess tissue lessened the efficiency of the physical machine which was the body, but Yoka was skeletal in his thinness. Beneath the scarlet robe, his body was reed-frail, his throat a match for the gaunt face and sunken eyes which, with his shaven pate, gave his head the appearance of a skull. A skull set with the jewel of his eyes which burned now, as always, with the steady flame of trained and directed intelligence.

He said, "No, Cyber Irae, the flowers are here to set at ease those ushered into this chamber to wait. Naturally, you grasp the underlying purpose."

A statement, not a question. For him to have framed the sentence otherwise would have been tantamount to insult. No cyber could avoid seeing the obvious, and now that Irae knew the purpose of the room, the presence of the blooms and the position they occupied was plain. A contrast and a good one; outside, the bleak desolation of Titanus—within, the glowing color and beauty of the flowers and what they, by association, represented. The security of the Cyclan; the rewards and wealth and comfort the organization could provide to any who engaged their services. A contrast too subtle to be immediately appreciated by any visitor, but it was there and would be noted on a subconscious level.

"Caradoc shows skill and intelligence. An acolyte?"

"No longer." Yoka lifted a hand and touched his breast, fingers thin and pale against the rich scarlet and the design embroidered on the fabric. A gesture signifying the acolyte had passed his final tests and was now one of their number. Beneath his hand the Seal of the Cyclan glowed and shimmered with reflected light. "A young man who shows promise. He should give good service and rise high."

And would, unless he committed the unpardonable crime of failure.

Irae looked again at the flowers, at the window and the desolation beyond, thinking of others who had shown promise and who had failed. Those who had paid with their lives because of their failure. Others who had been broken. He did not intend to become one of them.

He said, "You are certain Dumarest is not on this world?"

"I am."

"The prediction that he could be found on Titanus was of seventy-three per cent probability."

"Not high."

"No, and obviously there were factors we could not take into account. Even so, we must be close."

As they had been close before, each time to miss the quarry by a few minutes of time, by coincidence, by the luck which seemed to follow Dumarest from world to world. A trail marked by the death of cybers he had killed in order to ensure his escape.

The irrevocable loss of trained and dedicated intelligences which should have gone to swell the complex of Central Intelligence.

The reward of every cyber who proved his worth.

"It is against all logic," said Yoka. "How could one man have eluded capture for so long?"

Luck, and more than luck. The instinct which gave warning when danger was close. The intelligence which recognized the threat and remained alert for the little things which gave warning—a stare maintained too long, a glance, a too-fortuitous meeting, a proffered friendship, an unexpected invitation—who could tell?

And yet, the Cyclan should be able to tell. The cybers, with their trained minds which could take a handful of known facts and from them extrapolate the logical sequence of events encompassing any imaginable variation. To arrive at a deduction and make a prediction which was as close as possible to actual prophecy. They should know where a man on the move would come to rest, had known, but still he had managed to dodge, to stay one jump ahead.

For too long now. Too long.

Irae studied the flowers. Had an insect hummed among the blossoms he would have been able to predict on which it would next settle, on the pattern it would follow. Had he wanted to snare it, he would have known exactly where to apply the compound which would hold it fast.

An insect—why not a man?

He said, "We know that Dumarest is among the worlds of the Rift. That is a probability of ninety-nine percent. We have checked the course of each vessel leaving relevant worlds and have agents alerted at each port of call. All precautions have been taken."

And still they hadn't proved enough. Like a ghost, Dumarest had vanished, aided by the unpredictable, riding his luck until even those searching for him had begun to doubt their powers.

"The Rift," said Yoka. "A good place for a man to hide."

Too good. A section of space in which suns burned close and worlds were plentiful. An area in which opposed energies created dangerous vortexes and regions in which matter itself could cease to exist. A place in which planets rested in isolation in whirls of dust, rolled hidden in masses of interstellar gloom, hung like glittering gems in a web of destructive forces. A haystack in which a wisp of straw could so easily be lost.

Irae lifted his eyes from the bowl of flowers and turned like a scarlet flame to where Yoka stood respectfully waiting.

"Your conclusions?"

"Based on all available data, the probability of capturing Dumarest at this time is fifty-three percent. Not until he is located can we hope to gain information on which to base a more favorable prediction."

"Fifty-three percent?"

"Low," admitted Yoka, "but I said 'capture,' not 'discover'. The probability of spotting him is higher—seventy-six percent."

"Eighty-seven point five," corrected Irae. "You are too conservative. Even if he is now in space he must eventually land and when he does, an agent could spot him."

"If the man is at the right time, at the right place." Yoka had the stubbornness of age. "It comes to a matter of logistics. In order to maintain surveillance at every probable port of call at all appropriate times, we need the services of an army of men. Add to that the probability that he is on a planet and, unless he makes a move, locating him will be far from easy. And we must check all worlds." He ended, "In the Rift they are many."

He said it without change of the smooth, even modulation, devoid of all irritant factors which all cybers were trained to adopt. And yet, Irae caught the irony beneath the apparently flat statement.

"You repeat the obvious, Cyber Yoka. I am fully aware of

the problem but we can eliminate a large area of low-order probabilities. We have information as to where Dumarest was last located, together with the names and routes of the vessels which left at the critical time."

"Data?" Yoka stood, immobile, as he listened to the stream of facts and figures, his mind assimilating, correlating, selecting and discarding various possibilities until he reached a decision. "You are correct. The probability that Dumarest will be discovered within the Rift is as you say. The Quillian Sector. He could be there now, but to locate him will not be easy."

"For a cyber?"

"For anyone but an expert hunter of men." Yoka added, "I have one at hand."

Leo Bochner didn't look the part. While tall, he appeared slim, almost womanish, his face unlined, his hands smooth, as was his voice as he announced himself. He stood waiting with an easy grace. Instinctively, he selected the one in authority, turning a little to face Irae, recognizing that while younger than Yoka, he held the command. A point Irae noted as he did the clothing; good, yet not obtrusive; fine woven cloth cut to emphasize good taste and not vulgar ostentation. Clothing which somehow added to the effeminate impression he had gained and which lessened the threat of the man.

A mistake?

A less experienced man could have thought so and wondered at Yoka's judgement, but Irae had long since learned to look beneath the surface of apparent truth. Now, looking, he noted the smooth pad of muscle beneath the skin of face, throat and wrists. The iron beneath the smooth set of lips and jaw. The carriage. The ingrained confidence in words and manner. The eyes.

The eyes which, even as he watched, changed to give the lie to the polished dress and manner; turning into those of a beast, a wolf, a tiger, a hunter of prey.

Then, in a moment, they were again a part of the disguise, calm, bland, faintly mocking.

Irae said, "Tell me something of yourself."

"I have, shall we say, a certain skill." Bochner's voice carried no pride, it was merely a vehicle used to convey a fact. "I realized I had it when very young and took steps to culti-

vate and perfect it. I have an affinity with wild things. I sense
their habits and, knowing them, can anticipate what they will
do." He added with the same easy tone, "I am probably the
finest hunter ever to be born on Pontia, and on that world
you hunt or you starve."

"Animals." Irae watched the eyes as he spoke. "Beasts operating on instinctive patterns of behavior."

He had looked for anger. None came, nor did the eyes
change as they had before. That, he knew, had been a
demonstration, a dropping of the veil to show a little of the
real nature of the man.

Bochner said, "Beast or man, my lord, they are the same."

"A man can think."

"And for that attribute, has lost others. But we talk to little
purpose. My record is known to you."

A good one or he would not now be standing before them.
A noted hunter, a skilled assassin, but this time such skills
would be unwanted.

Bochner shrugged as Irae made that clear.

"I understand. I find Dumarest and hold him with the least
amount of force necessary until he can be handed over to
your agents. Of course, it may be that I shall have to cripple
him to ruin his mobility. Break his legs, for example, and
even his arms. But his life will not be in danger. That is ac-
ceptable?"

"We want the man unharmed and in full possession of his
mental faculties."

"You want the man in any way he can be delivered," said
Bochner flatly. "As long as he is alive on delivery. If that
isn't the case, why send for me?" His eyes moved from one
to the other of the scarlet figures. "I shall not let you down,
my lords. My reputation was not gained by bungling my
commissions. And, speaking of commissions my fee—"

"Will be paid," said Yoka. "The Cyclan does not break its
word."

A bow was Bochner's answer, but Irae added more; it was
well that the man should remember the power of the Cyclan,
and that it could take as well as give.

"You will be rewarded," he said, "with wealth and
property should you succeed. With something less pleasant
should you fail."

"I shall not fail."

"How can you be sure? How can you even know you will find him?"

"When you cannot?" Bochner was shrewd. "Or when you do, you always seem to arrive too late? The answer is basically simple; you hunt a man but I hunt a beast. You operate on the basis of pure logic, but a man is not a logical creature and does not follow a nice, neat, predictable path. Not a man with sense. Not one who knows he is being hunted. Not one who is afraid. Such things confuse the normal pattern. Watch such a man as I have and you will see his instincts guide his decisions. A ship arrives—shall he take it or wait for the next? The same with a raft, a cab, a caravan. The same with a hotel, a meal, a drink in a tavern. The shape of a door can send quarry scuttling into hiding. The whisper of a woman who, by chance, speaks his name. The look of an official which, misunderstood, can lead to flight. How can you predict exactly where he will go when he doesn't even know himself? What he will do, when what he is permitted to do depends on chance?"

He was over-simplifying and was wrong in his assessment of the ability of the Cyclan, but Irae did not correct him. Neither he, nor any cyber, wished to advertise their abilities to those who had not hired their services. And the 'chance' to which Bochner referred was not a matter of infinite variables, as he seemed to think, but a limited set of paths determined by prevailing factors. A man stranded on an island could only escape by sea or by air. Without the means to fly, he was limited to the sea. Without the means to construct or obtain a boat, he could only swim. If unable to swim, he would be forced to wade the shallows. Knowing the man, the circumstances, there was nothing hard in predicting what he would do and where he would go.

Irae said, "Do you know the Quillian Sector?"

"As much as any man can know it."

"Which is to say?"

"Parts well, other parts not so well, a little not at all. But then," Bochner added, "no one knows them—the worlds hidden in the dust and those caught in the mesh of destructive forces. There are rumors, but that is all."

"Expeditions sent and lost," said Yoka. "Companies formed and dissolved, as the investigations they made turned to nothing. We are not interested in such planets. We are only interested in your quarry."

"Dumarest"

"Yes, Dumarest. You are confident you can track him down?"

"Guide me to a world and if he is on it, I will find him. More, give me a cluster of worlds and I will show you which he will make for. You think I boast?" Bochner shook his head. "I speak from knowledge. From conviction. From experience."

"A claim others have made. Now, they are dead."

"Killed by Dumarest?" Bochner looked at his hands. "I can take care of myself."

A conviction shared by others before they had. died, but Irae didn't mention that. Instead, he said, "Tell me one thing, Bochner. Aside from the reward, why do you want to hunt Dumarest?"

"Why?" Bochner inhaled, his breath a sibilant hiss over his teeth. "Because if half of what you've told me is true, then he is the most wily, the most dangerous and the most interesting quarry I could ever hope to find."

The ship was small, unmarked; The crew, taciturn servants of the Cyclan. Alone in his cabin, Bochner went through his routine exercises, movements designed to keep his muscles in trim and his reflexes at their peak. When Caradoc opened the door he was standing, dressed only in pants, shoes and blouse, a knife balanced on its point on the back of his right hand, which was held level at waist height. As the young cyber watched, he dropped the hand and, as the knife dropped towards his foot, snatched at it with his left hand, catching the hilt and tossing it upwards to circle once before catching it in his right.

"A game," he explained. "One played often on Vrage. There we stood naked and held our hands at knee height. Miss and you speared a foot. There was a more sophisticated version played for higher stakes in which, if you were slow, you usually died." Idly, he spun the knife. "You have used a blade?"

"No."

"You should. The feel of it does something to a man. Cold, razor-sharp steel, catching and reflecting the light, speaking with its edge, its point, words of threat and pain. Watch a man with a knife and see how he moves. A good fighter becomes an appendage of his weapon. A man with a gun gives less cause for concern. Why? Can you tell me why?"

"A gun is dispassionate. Everyone knows what a knife can do."

"Cut and slash and maim and cripple. True, but a gun can do that and more. But still the psychological factor remains." Then in the same tone of voice he added, "Is that why Dumarest carries a knife?"

"You have read the reports."

"Words on paper—what do they tell me about the man? I need to know how he looks, how he walks, the manner in which he snuffs the air. You think I joke? Smell is as important to a man as to a beast, even though he may not be aware of it. And a man hunted and knowing it seems to develop his faculties. So what is Dumarest really like?"

"I have never seen him."

"He wears gray, he carries a knife, he travels. High when he can afford it, low when he cannot. Space is full of such wanderers. What makes him so special?" It was a question to which he expected no answer, and gained none. Either Caradoc didn't know or had no intention of telling, but it was early yet and, later—who could tell? Gesturing to his bunk, he said, "Sit and join me in some wine."

"No," said Caradoc.

"No to the wine, to the offer of rest, or both?"

"I need neither."

A thing Bochner had known but had deliberately ignored, Caradoc was a cyber and the nearest thing to a living machine possible to achieve. To him, food was mere fuel to power the body. He was a stranger to emotion and unable to feel it by virtue of the operation performed on his cortex shortly after reaching puberty. A creature selected and trained by the Cyclan, converted into an organic computer, a metabolic robot who could only know the pleasure of mental achievement.

Sitting, Bochner stared at him, wondering what it would be like to have been like him, to have worn the scarlet robe, to have relinquished all the things which most men held dear. Caradoc would never know the thrill of sitting in a hide waiting for the quarry to appear, to aim, to select the target, to fire, to know the heady exultation of one who has dispensed death. The sheer ecstasy of pitting mind against mind in the hunt for one of his own kind—the most exciting and danger-ous quarry of all. To kill and to escape, which often was harder than the kill itself. To outguess and outmaneuver. To anticipate and to watch the stunned sickness in a quarry's eyes. To hear the babble for mercy, see the futile twitches as the demoralized creature tried to escape, to plan even while it begged to die, finally, when the hunter had become bored.

No, Caradoc would never know what it was to be bored and for that alone, Bochner could envy him.

The wine was in a bottle of crusted glass, the crystal flecked with inner motes of shimmering gold, the liquid itself a pale amber, holding the tart freshness of a crisp, new day. Bochner poured and lifted the cap which served as a cup.

"To your health, my friend." He drank and refilled the small container. "You object?"

"I wonder."

"Why I drink?"

"Why any man of intelligence should choose to put poison into his body."

"A good point," mused Bochner. "Why do we do it? To find escape, perhaps to discover a world of dreams. Some cannot do without the anodyne of alcohol, but I am not one of them. Listen, my scarlet accomplice, and try to compre-hend. The quarry I hunt lurks in unsuspected quarters and must be sought in regions you may not understand. At times, I must sit for long hours in taverns and what should I drink then? No, I drink as a part of my camouflage and must maintain my tolerance for alcohol. As a runner must prac-tice to keep up his acquired ability. A swimmer, his mastery over water." Again he emptied the cup and again refilled it. "Test me now and you would find me as sober as yourself. Give me a mark and a gun and I will hit it as many times as you choose to name. In any case, it helps to pass the time."

"Quick-time will do that better."

"The drug will shorten the days and little else." Bochner slowly finished his wine. "But no compound ever yet discov-ered or invented can ease the weight of boredom."

An alien concept which Caradoc could understand only on an intellectual level. How could anyone ever grow bored in a universe filled with an infinity of questions awaiting answers? Even the cabin in which they sat offered endless scope for mental exercise connected with its structure, stress factors, cubic capacity, resonance, relationships of planes and divergencies from the mathematical norm.

Bored?

No cyber could ever be that while two atoms remained to pose a problem of interrelationship proximities. While life remained to set the eternal question of what and why it existed at all.

But lesser beings needed the convenience of quick-time; the drug which slowed the metabolism so that normal days passed in apparent minutes. A means to lessen the tedium of ship life on journeys between the stars.

The steward brought it an hour later when the vessel was aligned on its target star and safely on its way. He nodded to Caradoc and, without a word, lifted the hypogun he carried, aimed it at Bochner's throat and pressed the release. Air blasted the charge through skin, fat and muscle directly into the bloodstream. Bochner should have immediately turned into the rigid semblance of a statue. Instead, he slumped and fell unconscious on the bunk.

"Minimum dose as ordered, sir," said the steward. "Another?"

"No. You have all that is necessary? Good. Stand aside while I work."

Caradoc turned the unconscious man on his back, handling the bulk with surprising strength. From a packet the steward handed him, he took a slender instrument and a small capsule together with a can of anesthetizing spray fitted with a slender nozzle. Thrusting the nozzle into Bochner's right nostril, Caradoc hit the release, numbing and sterilizing the inner membranes. With the instrument, he quested the nasal passage and located the entrance to the sinus cavity. Removing the instrument, he fitted the capsule to its end, thrust the small package into the nostril, pressed and pushed it into the sinus. There it expanded, thin filaments attaching themselves with minute hooks to the inner lining, they and the capsule both coated with numbing and sterile compounds.

As he withdrew the spray after a final treatment Caradoc said to the steward, "Now. Neutralize and administer quick-time."

A metabolic shock, but Bochner was fit and could stand it, and what did it matter if the jar to his system should have later repercussions? He was a tool to be used for the benefit of the Cyclan and nothing more. The instrument planted within his skull was a device which, on receiving a signal, would respond with a burst of coded emissions. No matter where or how he tried to hide, he could be found, and the capsule itself could be exploded by remote control.

No one living had ever betrayed the Cyclan and Bochner would not be the first.

Caradoc watched as the steward set him upright, deftly triggering the hypogun, seeing the slow movements of the hunter's hands and eyes. Movements which jerked to normal as his own metabolism responded to the impact of the drug blasted into his bloodstream. The door blurred and they were alone.

Bochner wished he was more so. He hadn't wanted the company of the cyber but had known better than to protest Irae's decision. Later, if the need arose, he would slip away and certainly, if necessary, the cyber would have to change his appearance. The scarlet robe and naked scalp were signals the quarry couldn't miss.

Thinking of the hunt, he said, "How can you be so sure he is within the Quillian Sector?"

"Dumarest?" Caradoc leaned back to rest his shoulders against the wall. Bochner had noticed nothing wrong and that was proof of his own efficiency. He sat as Bochner remembered, the cabin looked the same. To Bochner, his temporary unconsciousness would have seemed no more than the blink of an eye. "A matter of applied logic."

"A guess?"

"No."

"And yet you can't be certain. I mean, you might know about where he is but not exactly where. If your logic and skill were good enough surely there could be no doubt?"

"Doubt?"

"Uncertainty. You would be certain."

"Nothing is ever that," said Caradoc. "Always there is the unknown factor which must never be ignored. No matter how certain a thing appears to be, it must never be considered an absolute event. The probability may be high but, always, it remains a probability."

Bochner nodded, remembering a time during his early youth. A copse in which a beast was lurking, himself set and armed, the weapon lifted, aimed, the butt hard against his shoulder, the sights leveled on the spot in which the creature was sure to appear. A long, delicious moment of savored anticipation. The nearing climax of the hunt was like the climax of sex itself, though far more satisfying.

And then the shadow, which had crossed the sun. The raft, which had appeared in a cloudless sky and, as it threw a patch of darkness over the front sight, the quarry had appeared to turn, to run, to dodge the bullet which should have brought it low.

Revenge had done little to ease the hurt and after the dead man had toppled from the raft, and the vehicle itself risen to vanish into the distance, the penalty had waited at the end— the blood-price paid in money and sweat and exile from his home world.

A little thing. One he should have taken into consideration. A neglect which had altered the trend of his life.

Watching him, Caradoc said, "Imagine a container of boiling liquid containing tiny motes of solid substance. They are in continuous, restless activity. The Brownian Movement. The tiny particles are in motion because of the irregular bombardment of the molecules of the surrounding medium. Now, imagine one of the particles to be colored for easy identification. We can tell where it is in relation to the whole. We can tell where it has been. We can even predict where next it might be, but never can we be utterly and absolutely certain."

"Dumarest? The colored particle is Dumarest?"

"The analogy will serve."

"And you know about where he is to be found. In the Quillian Sector." Bochner's face became taut, ugly, the skin tightening so that his cheeks looked like scraped bone. "The place where space goes mad. Where the suns fight and fill the universe with crazed patterns of energy so that men kill at a glance and women scream at imagined terrors. Ealius and Cham and Ninik."

"Swenna," said Caradoc adding to the list. "Vult and Pontia—" He paused, then said again, "Pontia."

"Where I was born." Bochner's voice matched the taut ugliness of his face. "I told you I knew the area well."

Chapter Two

Dumarest heard the shout and looked up to see death falling from the sky. The grab of the digger was overhead, the jaws open, tons of oozing clay scooped from the cutting, blotting out the pale orange of the firmament. It should have been neatly deposited in the body of his truck. Instead, it was plummeting down to crush and bury him. No accident. The crane was well to one side, the truck closer to it than himself, but there was no time to think of that.

Even before the warning shout had died he was on the move, lunging to one side, feeling his foot slip on the loose dirt, toppling off-balance as the load thundered down.

Luck was with him. A second later, or had he been less fast, he would have been crushed and buried like an insect. As it was, he felt the impact on his left shoulder, the barest touch of the debris which rasped down the sleeve of his coverall, the blow throwing him further in the direction of his fall. He hit a slope, rolling, falling, to land on the water-logged clay at the foot of the cutting as over him showered the mass of clay, dirt and rubble.

Too much rubble. It pressed on his back, drove his face into the water as it piled on his head, his shoulders, trapping his entire body with a layer of dirt which pressed with an iron hand. A hand which could kill, which would kill within minutes unless he could find some way to breathe.

He strained, body aching, muscles tense, blood thundering in his ears as, slowly, he lifted. A fraction only; loose dirt compacted by his upward pressure, yielding a trifle to form a shallow gap beneath him so that, arms and legs rigid, back arched against the strain, head turned to rest one cheek in the water, his nose lay above the surface and he could breathe.

Breathe and wait for a rescue which need never come.

Life was cheap on Ealius. Only the skilled technicians were of value, the rest were easily replaced. Those in authority could decide that he wasn't worth the trouble and effort to save. Better to let him lie, to be covered in, buried, forgotten. But the cutting had to be kept open, the great channel formed and smoothed, the passage through the mountain maintained.

After what seemed hours, Dumarest felt and heard the grating vibration of mechanical jaws.

They were not being operated with any care for the vulnerability of a human body. The steel teeth dropped, closed, lifted with a load of clay to set it aside and return for more. Only a concern to avoid marring the sides of the channel made the operator take small bites at the mound he had dropped. The fact that any of the scoops could have sheared through a body didn't seem to have occurred to him.

Dumarest had a more personal interest. He felt a touch against one leg, kicked, felt metal beneath his foot and then the rasp of the teeth over his thigh. Luck had saved him; a few more inches and his foot would have been caught, his leg ripped from its socket as the grab lifted with resistless force. Before it could return he heaved, squandering the last of his conserved energy, fighting the crushing weight on back and shoulders as he thrust himself back to where the clay had been lifted from his legs. When next the grab returned, he was ready. As the open jaws dug into the mound he threw himself into the grab, ducking as the serrated edges closed, one hand caught between two of the steel teeth of the low jaw, the upper halting an inch from his wrist as it closed on a stone.

Then up and out to one side, the grab halting, turning, opening as it jerked to shower its load into the open body of the truck waiting below. As Dumarest fell, he heard a yell.

"It's Earl! By damn, it's Earl!"

Carl Devoy, the one who had shouted, his face taut beneath a tangle of rust-colored hair now smeared with ocher clay. He ran to the side of the truck, heaving himself up and staring over the side.

"Earl?" He sucked in his breath as Dumarest moved. "By God, he's still alive! Give a hand here! Give a hand!"

He was small, but with a temper to match the color of his

hair, and two men ran to obey. A third arrived with a bucket
of water as they lowered Dumarest to the ground and, without preamble, threw the contents over the clay-smeared figure.

"Earl?"

"I'm all right." Dumarest straightened, breathing deeply,
water running down his head and face to soak his coverall.
As he wiped his hands on his sides, he said, "Who was operating the digger?"

"Menser. He's still operating it." Devoy glanced at the man
seated in the cab of the machine. A transparent canopy gave
weather-protection, its clarity now marred with dirt. Behind
it, the face and figure of the operator were blurred. "I saw
the bucket jerk and yelled but I was too late."

"No," said Dumarest. "If you hadn't shouted I'd be dead
now. And then?"

"After the load dropped?" Devoy shrugged. "They figured
you had to be dead and would have left you but Strick
wanted the cutting to be cleared. Ten minutes later and he'd
have left it for the next shift to clear up the mess."

Ten minutes—the difference between life and death.
Dumarest looked at the orange sky, at the bulk of the digger
etched against it, at the dark face which peered at him from
behind the canopy. As a whistle blew the face moved, became a part of the body which climbed down from the cab, a
man who stood almost seven-feet tall and with shoulders to
match. A black giant with massive hands and thighs like
trees. A man who stepped to where Dumarest stood waiting,
to halt, to part his lips in a grin before spitting on the
ground.

"Mister, you were lucky."

"No," said Dumarest. "You were careless."

"Meaning the accident?"

"If it was one."

"Hell, man, how can you doubt it? A cable locked and I
had to snap it clear. That's why I swung the grab over and
away from the truck. Sometimes the catch slips and you drop
the load."

"On me?"

"I didn't see you." Menser spat again. "I had other things
to think about."

Truth or lie, there was no way of telling and certainly

nothing could be proved. Dumarest studied the man, seeing the eyes, white rims showing around the irises, the corners tinged with red. The telltale signs of the drug he chewed, as was the purple spittle he had vented on the ground. The pungent, shredded leaf which gave euphoria at the cost of sanity.

Then, as the whistle shrilled again, Devoy said, "Come on, Earl, let's get away from here. The next shift's taking over."

The residential quarters matched the workings; hard, rough, severely functional. Sleeping was done in dormatories, eating in a communal mess, washing in a long, low room flanked by shallow troughs above which showers supplied water ranging from tepid to steaming hot. The place itself was filled with steam; writhing vapor which blurred details in a manmade fog. In it shapes loomed, indistinct, voices muffled as men called to each other.

Stripped, Dumarest stepped under a shower, feeling the drum of water on his head, the rivulets cleaning away the grime and dirt from his hair. Soap came in liquid form from a dispenser and he filled his palm with the sticky goo, rubbing it hard and getting little result.

"Here, Earl, try this." Devoy handed over a bar of soap from where he stood in the adjoining shower. "Something special from a friend in town." His wink left no doubt as to the nature of the 'friend'. "She likes her men to smell nice. Go ahead," he urged. "It's good."

The soap held a crude perfume but it contained oil and lacked the harsh bite of the supplied liquid. Dumarest used it, creating a mass of suds which flowed over the firm muscles of shoulders and back, stomach and thighs. As he turned beneath the shower to wash them free, Devoy sucked in his breath.

"Hell, Earl, you look as if you'd been clawed by a giant."

Dumarest turned to examine his legs. On the back of each calf, running midway up each thigh, ran a wide, purpling bruise: the result of the raking jaws of the grab. They marred the hard, smooth whiteness of the skin, as did the other marks carried on his chest and forearms, the thin cicatrices of old wounds.

Devoy looked at them, recognizing them for what they were, wondering why he hadn't spotted them before. The long bruises gave the answer to that; unless they had caught his attention he wouldn't have stared. Wouldn't now know that Dumarest bore the scars of a man who has fought with naked blades. That he was a fighter, trained to kill.

He said, "That's Menser's trouble, Earl. I've heard it from others in the gang. He's been pushing, seeing how far he can go, how much he can get away with. That accident could have been fixed."

"I know."

"Does he have anything against you? Did he try to push and you told him where to get off?"

Dumarest shook his head, then lifted his arms to let the steaming water cascade over his body, the impact helping to ease the ache of muscles recently overstrained. Since coming to the workings he had kept himself to himself, not asking for trouble, not looking for it. The last thing he wanted was to become the center of attention. Now, it seemed, Menser had other ideas.

He came into the washroom, voice booming, attended by a handful of sychophants eager to hook their wagon to a profitable star. On any construction site there were men who recognized opportunity when they saw it and took steps to skim the cream. Parasites, using threats and violence to intimidate others, demanding a share of their pay under the guise of collecting contributions, donations, or as insurance premiums. Such men, if they survived, could become rich and powerful with their own small, private armies to enforce their dictates.

Menser wanted to become one of them.

Dumarest watched as the steam swirled to part, to reveal the giant, to close again over his giant frame. What the man did was no concern of his as long as he was left alone, but Menser had recognized in Dumarest a source of potential trouble. To eliminate him would pay dividends in more ways than one.

"He's high," said Devoy uneasily. "Doped and crazed and spoiling for trouble. Let's get out of here."

Good advice, but Dumarest didn't follow it. If trouble was to come this was as good a place as any in which to meet it. He stood, the soap in his hand, eyes narrowed as he stared through the vapor. It broke, shredded, torn into wisps as the giant came forward, head lowered, shoulders hunched, fists pounding the air as, weaving, he shadowboxed his way along the edge of the trough. His intention was obvious; to locate his victim, to strike, to break bones and pulp flesh with hammer blows and then to explain that he had seen nothing in the steam and had maimed or killed by accident.

"Earl!" Devoy was anxious.

"Stand clear."

As the smaller man stepped from the shower, Dumarest left the trough to stand facing the approaching giant. Menser was huge, coiled ropes of muscle shifting beneath the gleaming ebon of his skin, his head a ball of bone, hair cropped close to the scalp. Now he looked up, grinning, a purple stream jetting from between his lips to spatter the floor inches from Dumarest's feet.

"Waiting for me, friend? Well, now, that's nice of you. A pity you're going to have another accident." His laughter was soft, feral, devoid of amusement. "A fatal one this time."

Dumarest threw the soap.

It flashed from his hand to drive against the giant's face, to land beneath one of the thick eyebrows and to slam against the eye with a force which tore the orb from its socket, to leave an ugly red hole streaming blood. A blow which shocked and blinded, one which he followed with another as, lunging forward, he lifted his foot and sent the heel up hard against the chin.

It was like kicking a mountain.

Menser yelled, one hand lifting to his ruined eye, the hand falling as he dodged Dumarest's second kick. Hurt, he was even more dangerous than before, pain fueling the hate now powering his muscles, obliterating everything but the desire to rend and kill the man standing before him. Like an oiled machine, he swung into action, hands extended, feet moving in little, dancing steps, body poised to turn in any direction.

A wrestler and a dangerous one. A man with a very high pain threshold, as his apparent ignoring of his ruined eye testified. One who had to be treated with respect and caution.

One Dumarest had to kill before being killed.

He moved back, aware of the circle of watchers, the eyes avid with anticipation, the faces gloating at the free and unexpected spectacle. Faces rendered more beastlike by the blurring vapor, eyes more feral because of the steam.

"You bastard!" Menser inched forward. "I was just going

to hurt you a little, break a few bones, maybe, or give you some bruises. Now I'm going to make you pay for what you did. Your eyes first, maybe. Or maybe I'll smash both legs and, as you crawl, tear out your arms. Then I'll take care of your eyes, a thumb in each socket, pressing slowly, so slowly, until they pop out like stones from a fruit. And then—"

His voice whispered on but Dumarest ignored it. A trick to command a part of his attention and to ruin a little of his concentration. To weaken him by fear and to soften him by imagined terrors. Blatant tactics he had long since learned to disregard.

"Earl! Get him, Earl! Get the bastard!"

Carl Devoy offering what help he could and at the same time revealing both his courage and stupidity. If Menser should win he would be marked and taken care of—a high price to pay for the encouragement Dumarest didn't need.

He dropped as the giant came in, turning, his hand rising to chop with stiffened palm at the man's left knee. He felt the jar and spun to one side as the right foot lashed at his face, kicking back in turn, his heel impacting the knee he had struck. Then he was up and on his feet, circling to keep on the blind side of his opponent, making use of the advantage he had won.

A fist darted toward him, to scrape against the side of his head as he weaved, the forearm like an iron bar as he gripped it, throwing back his weight, trying to throw the giant off-balance. Menser yielded, snarled as his other hand grabbed, laughed as the fingers sank into Dumarest's shoulder.

"Now," he gloated. "Now!"

His knee jerked upwards, Dumarest turning to avoid the crippling impact, striking back in turn, his foot aimed at the same left knee. A weak blow, but one which added to the previously caused damage, and he followed it with a thrust of his head which hit the nose and sent more blood to join that streaming from the ruined eye.

Then Menser struck in turn.

His fist rose, darted forward, making a meaty impact as it slammed against Dumarest's torso. A blow aimed for the face, which had missed as Dumarest reared upwards, fighting the steellike fingers holding him fast. One followed by another, which brought stars flashing and the taste of blood. A third, which created a web of darkness which edged close as, all around, men yelled in anticipation of the kill.

Dumarest twisted, using his weight to tear free of the gripping fingers, sweat oiling his skin as he blocked another blow and sent his own hand to stab fingers in the ruined eye. Menser screamed, jumping back, hands lifted to protect his face as again Dumarest kicked at the knee. This time, he felt bone yield, the kneecap splintering, maiming the giant and robbing him of quick mobility. But even though he had to fight to maintain his balance, he still had his hands and the strength they possessed.

"Coward!" Menser snarled his hate as he stood balanced on one foot. "Come and fight like a man!"

An invitation only a fool would accept. Dumarest feinted, drew back and then, with a blur of movement, had run forward, his hands busy, stiffened palms like blunt axes as they drove at the throat, the windpipe and larynx, crushing both before he withdrew from the closing arms.

Again.

A third time, this one resulting in a long gash over his shoulder as Menser clawed at his elusive opponent.

And then again, to leave the giant sprawled like a fallen tree, blood puddling the floor around his mouth, one leg bent at an impossible angle, the great machine of his body broken and stilled.

The woman said quietly, "Hold on now, this is going to hurt."

Dumarest heard the rustling behind him as he lay prone on the couch, a shifting of clothing, a metallic rattle and then something like liquid fire traced a path over his shoulder.

As he grunted, the woman said, "You should have gone to the hospital."

"Aren't you a nurse?"

"I was once." Her tone held bitterness. "But that was a long time ago. Now I earn my living treating young fools who should have more sense than to get themselves hurt in stupid duels. We have a law against such things and the penalties are harsh. Hold still, now." Again came the liquid fire, the touch of acid burning away the corruption which had fes-

tered in the wound. Menser had carried vileness beneath his
fingernails; a paste containing virulent bacteria which, un-
treated, could kill. "There, that should do it. You were
lucky."

The woman was wrong. Caution, not luck, had dictated his
actions. He had noticed the festering gash and had suspected
its cause. The same caution had made him seek unofficial aid;
had caused him to leave the camp with pay still uncollected.
A precaution against Menser's friends and others who might
have agents lying in wait.

Now, turning, he looked at the woman who stood to one
side of the couch, a small bowl in one hand, the glass stylo
with which she had applied the acid held by her thumb.

"Is there anything else?"

"Maintain a watch on your temperature. Should it rise
more than five degrees take antibiotics and seek medical advice."

"The wound itself?"

"Has been cleaned and sealed. The compound of my own
devising; the residue film will peel automatically as the
wound heals." She added, "Is there anything else I can do for
you?"

He did not mistake her meaning even though she was still
attractive, though far from young. Many of those who paid
for her help would have wanted more than the service she offered—passion riding on the relief of assistance given. Perhaps she catered to them. People lived as best they could and
there was little charity on Ealius, but he sensed she had
judged him to hold wider interests.

"I need to get on a ship," said Dumarest. "I'd like to do it
without attracting attention. Would you know how it could
be done?"

"The gate is guarded," she said immediately. "All leavings
are checked against the files deposited by the construction
company. They don't want anyone leaving who owes them
money. Are you breaking a contract?"

"No."

"Then you could pass through the gate without difficulty."

"And if I were?"

"Breaking a contract?" She frowned. "There are ways if
you have money. Men who will smuggle you on a vessel as

long as you don't care where you go or how you end. I wouldn't advise using the service they offer."

"Why not?" Dumarest asked, but already knew the answer. Too many worlds close by had mines which needed workers and those who operated them were careless as to how they gained their laborers. A man, buying a secret passage, could wind up contracted to slave in a living hell. "What else is there?"

"If you can afford it, there are men who could arrange to have you signed on as a crew member."

"And would that be safer?" Dumarest eased himself from the couch. The sting had gone from the wound and he moved his arm a few times to test the pull of the plastic film covering it. "I'm avoiding enemies," he explained. "A little trouble I had—no need for detail. You've heard it all before."

As she had learned to recognize lies. As Dumarest dressed, she put away her things, turning to look as he donned the boots and the knife he carried in the right. They were a match for the pants and long-sleeved tunic, which rose high to fit snugly around the throat. Tough material in which was imbedded protective metallic mesh. The gray plastic was easy to clean and simple to refurbish. A convenience for any traveler.

As he reached for money, she said, "You paid me in advance."

"For the medical treatment only."

"The advice came free."

"And your silence?" He dropped coins on the couch as she made no answer. "This is to forget you've ever seen me. And this," he added more, "is for being what you are."

For not asking questions, for taking him in on the basis of nothing more than a whispered introduction from an intermediary, for taking care of the man, in turn. And, perhaps, for looking like someone else he had known years ago now, and a long journey through space. A woman who had tended him when, as a young man, he had suffered his first wound and who had healed the gash as she had tended his desires. Her name? That was forgotten, together with the name of the world on which they had met. But some things about her could not be forgotten; the touch of her hands, the shape of her hair, the clustered wrinkles at the corners of her eyes, her kindness.

"Thank you," the woman said quietly. She made no effort to pick up the money. "There is a tavern on the corner of North and Inner. Some captains and others have a habit of using the back room. Ask for Varn Egulus. But you are welcome to stay, if you wish."

"No. I must be on my way."

From the house and into the town and out to where the field lay in its circle of perimeter lights, with ships at rest and the stars winking like jewels against the black velvet of the sky. At the gate, men stood in casual attitudes, some uniformed with the garb of the local authority, others wearing ship uniforms, a few in civilian dress. Watching, Dumarest noticed how they examined a man coming toward them, how they checked him, watched after him when they allowed him to pass.

It could have meant nothing, but Menser could have been reported murdered and even if those watching had testified to the truth, personal combat was against the local regulations. He could be arrested, tried, fined or set to a term of forced labor. At best, it would mean delay.

"Mister!" One of the guards called to him. "You looking for something?"

"Yesh." He swayed, deliberately slurring his words, one hand pawing vaguely at the air as it hid his face. "A girl . . . she promised to meet me . . . late . . ." A hiccup emphasised his drunkenness. "Thish South and Outer?"

"No, you're on Inner and West. South is that way." A hand lifted to point, lowered as the guard turned away, losing interest but completing the directions. "Go up it and you'll hit Outer."

Dumarest lurched away, plunging deeper into the shadows, following directions until he was out of sight. Straightening, he turned up a narrow alley and made his way back to the road running north, turning to head back to the one curving around the field.

The tavern was like most of its type, a place where men journeying between the stars could find the comforts they lacked on their ships, the dissipations offered for their enjoyment. Dumarest shook his head as a pert young girl offered her invitation, shook it again as an older matron repeated it with added detail, shrugged as a man hinted at more exotic

delights. None was offended at his refusal, no recent arrival
could be considered a real prospect but it did no harm to try.
Later, when alcohol had worked its magic, or when drugs
had dulled the sharp edges of discrimination, they and others
would try again.

Varn Egulus was a tall man of middle age with a long,
serious face, a beaked nose and hair which was cut and lifted
in an elaborate forelock. His lips were thin, the jaw pro-
nounced, the cheeks hollowed as if with privation. Beneath
thin brows his eyes were shrewd, watchful, calculating.

He said, "It seems we have a mutual friend. Sit and order
some wine. Good wine—I can afford it since you are paying."

Dumarest obeyed, watching as the man poured, barely sip-
ping at what his own goblet contained. The woman must
have sent word ahead for Egulus to expect him and he would
take his own time in getting to the point.

"Good wine, this." Egulus lifted his glass and studied the
play of color trapped in the crystal. "Such a wine makes a
man glad to be alive." And then, without changing tone, he
said, "Why did you kill Menser?"

"Did I?"

"Perhaps not, but you match the description of the man
who did. The one who brought the news was most explicit as
to detail. He was also amazed at the speed you—the man—
operated. It was like watching the dart of lightning, he said.
Movements faster than the eye could follow." Egulus tilted
his goblet and slowly drank the wine it contained. Emptied,
he lowered it toward the table. Then, before it could hit the
surface, he flung it directly at Dumarest's face.

He smiled as it shattered on the floor.

"Clever," he mused. "You did not catch it as I thought you
might and, most certainly, could have done. You didn't simply block it, and so risk cuts to hand and face. Instead, you
deflected it as if by accident, to smash on the floor. Which
proves nothing to any who might be watching. Well, to
business.

"I command the *Entil*. A trader. One of the rules we follow is that nothing should ever be done without some form of
return. To do otherwise would be to operate at a loss and
only the stupid do that. A cooperative, you understand. We

work, take risks, carry any cargo we can get, and go any-where a profit is to be made."

And run a ship more like a heap of wreckage than a vessel designed to survive in the void. One that is undermanned, with faulty equipment and dangerous installations.

Egulus smiled again as he guessed Dumarest's thoughts.

"A ship such as you imagine wouldn't last long in the Rift. Also I have a regard for my life, which is why the *Entil* is as good as I can make her. But obviously, you've had experi-ence. What as? Steward? Handler?"

"Both."

"And?"

"I know a little about engines. A little more about caskets. And," Dumarest added, "I can operate a table should the need arise."

"A gambler?" Egulus pursed his lips as Dumarest nodded. "And one who can take care of himself if he has to. Good. That's an advantage. Now, this is the situation. You give me the cost of a double High passage and work as one of the crew. When you decide to quit, I'll compute what is your share of the profit and pay you off. Fair enough?"

For the captain, more than fair. Unless he was more hon-est than his fellows there would be no profits and he and the others would have gained passage money and service for nothing.

Dumarest said, "About the tables. What I win I keep?"

"You know better than that. It goes into the common fund."

"And if I lose?"

"You pay." The captain's tone hardened a little. "And I should warn you that I have no intention of haggling. The cost of a double High passage, take it or leave it. And I want the money now."

"No." Dumarest reached for the wine and called for a new goblet to replace the broken one. "You'll get it after I'm on the ship and we're on our way."

"You have it?" Egulus didn't wait for an answer. "You're committing suicide if you haven't. Unless I get paid, you'll be evicted into the void."

He meant it. Dumarest said, "Don't worry about the money. You'll get it. When do we leave?"

"At noon." Egulus reached for the wine Dumarest had

poured. "But we'll hit the gate an hour before dawn. The guards will be sleepy then. I'll arrange for a uniform for you before we leave here and they'll take you for one of my crew."

Chapter Three

The *Entil* was a pleasant surprise. Despite what the captain had claimed, Dumarest had expected to see the usual dirt and neglect of those sharing partnership and unwilling to perform more than the essential tasks. A ship run on a shoestring, with patches and stained paint and filters which passed dust and tanks which leaked air. He had worked on such vessels and traveled on them too often to have retained any illusions, but the *Entil* was the exception to the rule.

Dumarest checked it after Egulus had seen him aboard and then moved on to the control room. The passageway was brightly illuminated, the cabins opening on it clean and neat, the paint shining as if newly washed. The salon was well-furnished, the gaming table covered in clean, unworn baize, the light above throwing a neatly defined cone of brilliance. Testing the spigots, Dumarest found they not only supplied the normal water, but also a weakly alcoholic fruit drink. Unexpected luxury in any trader or in any vessel lower than the luxury class.

Allain, his guide, shrugged when he mentioned it. The steward was pushing middle age, his face smooth, bland with the diminution of curiosity. A man who had found his niche and who now observed the universe with cynical detachment and an extended palm.

"Egulus is smart. Advertise free wine and it adds the edge to persuading customers to ride with us instead of another. And it whets their appetites for something stronger."

"Which you can supply?"

"Naturally, and you, too." Allain glanced at the table. "Get them a little high and they get careless. A smart man

32

can really clean up if he puts his mind to it. Well, you'll learn. Now come and meet Jumoke."

Jumoke was the navigator. He was younger than the steward, with intense blue eyes and a mouth which betrayed an inner sensitivity. He rose from the edge of his bunk as Dumarest entered his cabin, extending his hand, lowering it as Dumarest touched the fingers. They were smooth and cool, the nails rounded and neatly polished.

He said, "So you have learned the old customs."

"On a world far from here, yes."

"The touching of hands," explained Jumoke to the steward. "A civilized act or an act performed among civilized peoples to show they have no hostile intent. On some worlds both hands are extended, on others only the empty palms are displayed." To Dumarest he said, "From Naud, perhaps?"

"No."

"Hagor, then? Fiander? Or even Grett? All three worlds use the old custom. Rumor has it they gained it from the Original People, but so often does rumor lie. Personally, I come from Vult. You know it?"

"The cesspool of the Rift," said Allain, before Dumarest could answer. "Every man is a thief or murderer, every woman a harlot, even the children learn to lie and cheat at their mother's knee. A world of madness."

"And our next port of call." Jumoke looked at the steward. "Aren't you supposed to be checking the stores?"

"It's done."

"Completely? You've checked the sensatapes? The rare and delicate wines? The stronger liquors? The preserved delicacies which fetch so high a price? Be careful, my friend. If, by your neglect, we lose a profitable sale, may God help you, for surely we shall not." Jumoke chuckled as the man hastily left the cabin. "He's good at his work but sometimes doubts his memory. Vult always disturbs him. Mention it and you get a tirade. He had a sister once—but never mind that now. We all have burdens to bear. Allain, myself, you—?" He paused then, as Dumarest made no comment, shrugged and smiled. "The captain mentioned you were close. But so close you are reluctant to give the name of your home world?"

"Earth."

"What?"

"Earth," said Dumarest again. The man was a navigator

and must have traveled far. And he could have heard the gossip of others of his kind. It was possible he had heard of the planet, knew where it was to be found. A hope which died as Jumoke laughed.

"A humorist! I knew you were a hard man but never that! Earth!" He laughed again. "You know as well as I that you talk of a legendary world. One of many—El Dorado, Bonanza, Jackpot, Avalon—the list is long. Myths invented by men yearning for paradise. Earth!" The navigator shook his head. "The name alone should warn you of its nature. Every world contains earth. They are made of it. Crops grow in it. Who would name a world after dirt?"

"It exists."

"In the mind."

"In space somewhere. It is real."

"Of course." Jumoke sobered, his tone gentle. "If you say so, my friend. Who am I to argue? We must talk more on the subject, but later. Now I have work to do in the control room; sensors to check and instruments to test. You understand?" Then, as he stepped toward the door of the cabin, he added, "A word of advice. The captain has little use for those who are less than serious. If he should ask about your home world, it would be best to lie a little. Tell him you were born on Ottery, for example. Or Heeg. They, at least, are in the almanac."

Outside, the passage was deserted. As Jumoke headed toward the control room, Dumarest moved in the other direction toward the hold and engine room. As handler, it was his job to check the stowing of cargo and to operate the caskets designed for the transportation of beasts and often used to carry those riding Low; people traveling doped, frozen and ninety percent dead, risking the fifteen percent death rate for the sake of cheap transportation.

Now the caskets were empty and the cargo, a mass of bales and metal-strapped boxes, already in place. Dumarest checked the restraints, tightening and adjusting as needed. More cargo could arrive before they left, but he doubted it. From what Egulus had told him, the main trade of the *Eltin* was in carrying passengers. Some of them could have personal luggage, and maybe personal packets of stores and cargo, but they would arrive with their owners.

Crouching, Dumarest checked the caskets, tracing the wires

and pipes, rising to swing open the transparent lids, closing them and operating the controls and watching the gauges showing the drop in temperature. As he lowered the lid of the last, he saw the woman standing in the open doorway leading to the engine room.

She was tall, with a helmet of glinting blonde hair, the tresses cropped to hug the head and to frame the wide, strongly boned face. The shoulders were wide, a support for the muscles supporting the prominent breasts which thrust unmistakable mounds beneath the tunic of her uniform. Her eyes were oval pools of vivid blueness, her ears small and set tight against the head, the nose a little uptilted above a generous mouth. The chin matched the cropped hair in its masculine determination and when she spoke, her voice held a deep resonance.

"Satisfied?"

"Number two needs some attention to the hinges."

"And?"

"Number four is sluggish on the intake."

"Full marks," she said. "Not many would have noticed that. At least you know your caskets. Ridden in them often?"

"Too often."

"It's a hell of a way to travel." Stepping forward, she extended her hand in Jumoke's gesture. Touching it, he found it soft yet firm and, now that he was close, he caught the scent of her perfume. It was floral, slightly pungent, accentuating her femininity but at variance with her general appearance. A sign that she was not attempting to emulate the male, perhaps. A personal touch which gave her an individuality, and rescued her from the anonymity of a uniform. "So you're the new man. Glad to have you with us. I'm Dilys Edhessa. The engineer. You?" She nodded as he gave his name. "Well, you're an improvement on Gresham. That's his uniform you're wearing. It's too tight at the shoulders and too loose around the waist, but I can fix that for you."

"What happened to him?"

"Gresham? He tried to hold out and was caught cheating by a couple of punters. Miners from Cham. He made the mistake of trying to get them and one shot him from under the table. You want to watch out for that, by the way. Make sure they keep their hands where you can see them. We carry some wild types, at times."

"And Gresham?"

"As I said, he'd been holding out on the common fund so when he got himself killed Varn wasn't too concerned. He took a bribe from the miners to forget what had happened and we dumped Gresham into the void." She made a gesture as if brushing dirt from her hands. "He was no loss."

"Anything else I should know?"

"I doubt it. You've met Jumoke and Allain? And you know the captain, of course. Now you've met me. That's the lot. We run the *Entil*. Including you, naturally."

An afterthought, and Dumarest could understand it. He, like the steward, was expendable. It would be natural for the woman to regard him as less important than herself. And with reason. Looking past her, Dumarest could see the humped bulk of the engines, the wink and gleam of instruments and monitors. A comforting sight; the neatness would extend to the maintenance of the all-important generator.

Following his eyes, she said, "Know anything about engines?"

"A little."

"Good, then you can help me run a check later on. Just routine, but it would help to have someone relay the readings. Someone who knows what it's all about." Then she added without change of tone, "Just in case you've tried a bluff with Varn, it won't work."

"I know that."

"Listen! What I'm trying to say is if you need a loan? You can pay it back later."

"Thank you, but it isn't necessary. I mean that."

"Good." She stood looking at him, her eyes level with his own. A woman as broad as himself but heavier due to the swell of hips, buttocks and breasts. An Amazon, but one who held an unmistakable femininity, whose eyes held a genuine concern. "I like the captain but, at times, he can be hard. As you can be, I guess. You have the look, Earl, the manner of—hell, what am I talking about?"

"The caskets," he said.

"What?"

"The hinges need fixing, as does the intake. If you'll let me have some tools, I'll take care of it."

"There's no hurry," she said, welcoming the change of subject, the path he had opened from the intensity of the moment when, startlingly, she had felt her body respond to his masculine closeness. "We don't use them often now. On most of the worlds we visit, it's easy enough for anyone to earn the cost of a High passage. And few are interested in traveling Low."

"But they wouldn't be refused if they asked?"

"Of course not. Why turn down a profit?"

"Then I'd better fix the caskets."

"We'll fix them," she corrected. "Together. But why the concern? If a man's too big a creep to gain the cost of a decent passage, why worry about him?"

He said dryly, "Call it a vested interest. That creep could be me."

From where he sat in the narrow confines of the cabin, Leo Bochner said, "In order to survive, an animal needs three essentials; food, shelter and seclusion. It must eat, have protection against the elements and, because no matter how strong or savage a predator it may be, it will need to sleep at times, and so be vulnerable." He helped himself to some of his amber wine. "A pattern which any hunter must bear in mind."

Caradoc said nothing, sitting with his face shrouded in the uplifted cowl of his robe, his hands buried within the wide sleeves. Bochner was a little drunk, or was trying to give that impression. If the former, he was betraying a weakness which could kill him; if the latter, then he must again be trying to get information. An exercise which the cyber would have found amusing if he had been able to experience the emotion.

"A pattern which has won me many a trophy," continued Bochner. "To learn the habits of the quarry, to trail, to anticipate and then, finally, to close in for the kill." His hand tightened around the cap of the ornate bottle. "To win and again affirm the superiority of a thinking mind."

"One fogged with drugs?"

"This?" Bochner lifted the cap and deliberately swallowed what it contained. "You object?"

"To your drinking, no. To the possibility of your failure, yes. Need I remind you that the Cyclan has little patience with those who fail? That when you accepted your present commission you also undertook certain obligations? It would be wise for you to remember them."

"Don't preach to me, Cyber!" For a moment the smooth, almost-womanish features changed, to become those of a feral beast, an animal devoted to the kill. "The Cyclans have hired my skill, nothing more. And why did they hire me? Why, with all the skills and talents you claim to possess, was it necessary to find another to hunt down the man you seek?" Leaning forward a little, he added, "Can't you, even now, guess why Dumarest has been able to elude you for so long?"

"Chance—"

"Luck! The whining excuse of fools!" Wine gurgled as Bochner refilled the little cup. "Shall I tell you why? You persist in thinking of Dumarest as a factor and not as a man. As a unit instead of a thinking, human being. You make your predictions and assess your probabilities and point to a certain place and claim that is the spot at which your quarry is to be found. Yet, the men sent there find they are too late, or get themselves killed, or discover that some incident has negated your prediction. And still you haven't trapped your prey, and still you can't understand why."

Caradoc watched as Bochner emptied his cup and again refilled it from the bottle.

"Dumarest is a man, not a cypher. An animal with sharpened instincts and an awareness of danger. But this time, he must know who is hunting him and why; an advantage he has which I do not. It would help if I did." Pausing, he waited, and Caradoc noted the steadiness of his hand, the absence of glimmering reflections from the glass of the bottle, the surface of the liquid in the cup. A pause which the hunter ended before it became obvious he waited for an answer. "But no matter how clever he is, the rules apply to him as they do to a beast. He has the same need for food, shelter and seclusion. Being human, all can be obtained with the one commodity— money. To get it he must steal, beg or work. To beg would take too long and bring too small a return. To steal is not easy, and to rob others is to take high risks for the sake of little gain. Therefore, he must work and where would a traveler without great skills obtain employment in the Quillian Sector? Work which would provide all a man in his position needs? Well, Cyber, where is he to find it? Where would he feel safe? Where else but among others of his own kind? Transients who ask no questions, employed by those who regard them as nothing but a needed source of labor. A con-

struction site—mines, roads, buildings, canals—but where,
Cyber? On which world?"

"Ealius. We arrive tomorrow."

They landed at sunset when the terminator was bisecting
the single continent and tattered clouds hung like shredded
garlands against the darkening orange of the sky. Bochner
paused at the gate as Caradoc went on his way, asking for
and receiving audience with the guard-commander, a burly,
sullen man who softened as money was pressed into his palm.

"Procedure? It's simple. We don't worry about arrivals and
only test people when they leave. We stand them on the detector and ask their names. If they lie, we hold them for further investigation. If they're on the list, the same."

"List?"

"Contract-breakers, debtors, those accused of any crime.
We catch them, hold them, pass them on for appropriate action. Dumarest?" He frowned. "No, no one of that name has
passed through."

"How can you be sure? Are you on duty at all times?"

"No, but we keep records and I check the lists. Want to
check?"

"I'll take your word for it. Sorry to have taken up your
time."

"Dumarest!" The commander frowned, musing. "Wait a
minute! Dumarest—that name's familiar." He turned to
where a man sat at a computer terminal. "Check it, Mallius."

A moment, then, "It's on the list, Commander. Man to be
detained if spotted. An accusation of theft by the Hafal-
Glych made on the—"

"Never mind that." The commander looked at Bochner.
"Satisfied?"

With the thoroughness of the Cyclan, if nothing else. The
listing of the name was proof of the efficiency of the organization—they must have alerted agents on every world in the
Quillian Sector to keep watch for Dumarest. His respect for
the man increased as he realized what difficulties he had to
face. Still had to face. A cunning and intelligent quarry who
should provide a stimulating chase.

Caradoc, sitting in a room in the foremost hotel, listened to
what he had learned, then said, "Your conclusions?"

"Dumarest must be working for one of the construction

companies here. Maybe the Fydale or the Arbroth—both are
large employers of labor.' '

"As is the Lenchief."

"You think that is where he is to be found?"

"The probability is high." Caradoc made a gesture of dismissal. "If you hope to gain your reward I suggest you waste
no further time. Contact me immediately if you have located
Dumarest. Once you are certain you have found the man I
will give you further instructions."

Bochner drew in his breath, aware of the rage mounting
within him, the anger which must surely burst to reveal itself
on his face. A rage triggered by the realization that the cyber
had already assessed all possibilities and had arrived at his
decision without deigning to consult his partner. His anger
was not helped by the knowledge that his inquiries at the gate
had been a waste of time.

Why hadn't he been told?

Caradoc said, "You have the name of the company and
can gain its location if you ask at the desk. They will also arrange for transportation. Is there more you need before un-
dertaking action?"

"No, I—" Bochner forced himself to remember that no cyber was ever sarcastic and that Caradoc's inquiry had been
genuine. "Aren't you coming with me?"

"There is no need. In fact, my presence could be a disad-
vantage. In any case, I have other work to engage my attention while you execute your commission." Again came the
gesture of dismissal. "Please delay no longer."

Caradoc followed the hunter with his eyes as the man left
the room. Bochner had mastered his obvious rage well and
that was to his credit, but against that was the fact there had
been no rational cause for anger at all. Another demonstration of the futility of emotion; the crippling reaction of the
mind and body to external stimuli which destroyed the sharp
reasoning power of the intellect. Had he considered the Cyclan to be so devoid of foresight that he had thought it necessary to question those at the gate? Had he no concept of the
power of the organization which had chosen to utilize his limited skills?

Yoka had chosen him, and the old cyber had long ago
proved his capabilities. Yet, too much importance should not
be placed on past achievements. Age could bring more than

physical decay; always there was the danger of a mind affected by senility. It was barely possible that all relevant factors had not been taken into account when he had decided on the use of Bochner. He would include the suggestion in his report. In the meantime, as he had mentioned to the hunter, he had other matters to attend to.

A touch on a button and a man answered the summons.

"Master!" The acolyte bowed. One of two sent from a different world on another vessel—what Bochner didn't know he couldn't guard against. "Your commands?"

"Send in Fan Dudinka."

He was of middle height, middle-aged, his face marked with lines of worry, his eyes wary even though his manner was assured. The Head of the Essalian Group, which faced ruin unless the Cyclan could help them.

"Cyber Caradoc, it is good of you to receive me."

"Please be seated." Caradoc waited until the man had taken a chair. "As you have been informed, your bid to engage the services of the Cyclan has been successful. Now it must be clearly understood by you, and those of your group, that I can take no sides, that I am not interested in matters of moral right or legal wrong, that my sole function is to predict the possibility of events resulting from nodes of action."

"And for that, we pay," said Dudinka. "But, unless we pay—" he swallowed, "for God's sake, what can we do?"

"The Essalian Group is composed of those who operate farms running along both banks of the Ess. The river will be diverted once the major cutting into the mountains is completed. Once that happens, then shortage of water will make the land unproductive." Caradoc lifted a hand to still the other's outburst. "I merely review the situation. Now, as to what you can do—your major crop is the narcotic weed used by many of the workers. It grows quickly, cures on the stem, can be harvested and shredded in a matter of weeks from initial planting."

"We could maintain production if we used hydroponic vats," said Dudinka, "but the cost would be prohibitive."

"And the returns nill. Once you raise your prices to compensate, you lose your market. Your problem is with the company digging the cutting. They have no real need to divert the river and could avoid it by constructing an appropriate channel. If you were to guarantee to meet the cost, the probability is ninety-one percent they would agree."

"We haven't the money."

"You have the crop. You could sell it to the company at a set price and deny all free sale. The profits the company would gain from a monopoly would more than compensate them for the expense of the channel." Caradoc added, "The probability they would accept such an arrangement is in the order of ninety-seven percent."

A simple solution to a basically simple problem—the more so when already the construction company had learned to rely on the advice given by the Cyclan. All would be satisfied and all would be eager, when the next problem rose, as it would when the workers left when the channel was completed, to hire again the services of a cyber. And the advice he gave would, as always, be slanted to dependency on the service offered by the Cyclan. Use it and gain wealth and security, and who dared not use it when a competitor might?

And, once a dependency had been achieved, it was only a step to later domination.

"Master?" The acolyte was at his side. "Is there anything you require?"

"No." Caradoc rose from his chair. "I shall rest for a few hours. Should Bochner call, summon me at once."

Fifty miles from the town, the hunter walked through a man-made jungle of rips and tears and steaming mounds of noxious vapors and tormented ooze, of patches of acid vileness and bogs of lurking dissolution. All construction sites were the same; places where nature had been ravaged, the earth torn, the area despoiled in order to wrest wealth or later gain with a casual disregard for the safety or comfort of those who toiled like insects beneath the sun by day and flood lights at night.

A good place in which a man could hide.

Or so a man on the run would think, not seeing beyond the immediate necessity of obtaining shelter and a degree of anonymity. But, in such places, no man was ever truly alone. Always eyes watched him; those of the gambling sharks eager to take his pay, of those who sold food and comforts, of the girls operating in the shacks at the edge of the perimeter; raddled harlots together with their pimps and the sellers of chemical dreams. Only in a city could a man be really alone, and only then if he had the money on which to survive. Without that, he would be forced to work however and wherever he could.

"Dumarest?" The man in the office shrugged. "Mister, they come and they go—how the hell can I remember a name? Check with the wages clerk."

"Dumarest?" The clerk scowled. "Do you realize how many we have working here? How long it will take me to hunt through the files? They get paid on the first of each month. Come back then."

"Dumarest?" A guard rubbed thoughtfully at his chin. "I can't place him. Say, why don't you ask among the girls?"

They knew nothing, and neither did the purveyors of killing delights. Bochner had expected little else. No quarry of any worth would leave so clear a trail or make such a stupid mistake. But he picked up a rumor and followed it, and spoke to a man who had a friend who knew a little more and who was willing to talk, once primed with a bottle.

"Dumarest? Tall, wears gray, doesn't say much? Yeah, I've seen him. Fact is, he got into a little trouble recently and killed a man. A fair fight, so I understand. Didn't see it myself, but I know who did."

"Dumarest?" Carl Devoy was cautious. "Never heard of him. The man who killed Menser? Well, he did a good job, the bastard asked for it, but I don't know who did it. Not Dumarest, you can take that as a fact. Who is he anyway, and why do you want him?"

The official in the morgue was curt.

"Menser? He had an accident. What business is it of yours?" Money mollified his tone. "Well, I guess it would do no harm to let you see him. You're lucky, we were going to dump him but the manager said to wait until dawn. He wanted to get the doctor's report. No doubt about it—accidental death."

An accident which had ruined an eye, broken a knee, crushed larynx and windpipe. Bochner examined the injuries, assessing the force which must have been used, the agility needed to escape the long arms. He checked the hands, the nails with their sharpened points, the paste beneath them. An animal and a dangerous one—how much more dangerous must be the one who had bested him?

Back in the town with a new day brightening the sky, he quested another jungle. One not as raw as the site, but as viciously alive with its own form of predators. Men whom he hunted down with the hard-won skill, the cunning learned over the years. Trees or houses, gutters or rivers, men or beasts, all were basically the same. Note your target, wait by the water hole, watch the feeding ground, the accustomed trail, and then close in for the kill. And if money takes the place of bullets, then it is that much easier.

All it took was time.

"Hurt?" The man had shifty eyes which never stared at any one thing for long. "A friend of yours? Hurt, you say?"

"Cut a little." Bochner winced as he moved his arm. "A quarrel that got out of hand—you know how it is."

"A friend?"

"That's what I said." Again Bochner winced as he moved. "A good friend. I'd like to help him."

"Then take him to the hospital."

"Which has doctors who'd ask questions, and guards who'd ask more. Hell, all I want is for someone to bind up a wound and I—my friend—can pay. For the service, and for anyone who guides him to it." Money sang its song of appeal as he dropped coins on the table between them. From the far side of the tavern a man stared, then rose and moved casually toward the door. Following the movement of the shifty eyes, Bochner said, "Him?"

"Yeah." The man snarled as a hand fell to grip his own as it tried to rake up the coins. To crush the flesh against the bone until blood oozed from beneath the nails. "What the hell are you doing? My hand!"

"Him?"

"I—to hell with it." The man whispered a name, gave directions. "You'll find help there but if you tell who told you—"

The man who had sauntered toward the door stepped forward as Bochner approached, fell back as stiffened fingers slammed into the pit of his stomach, again where the heart beat under the ribs. A precaution—but no hunter would allow himself to be hunted.

Afternoon found him with a woman who turned stubborn. At dusk, he had gained a name and had something which was barely alive. Before he left the house, he had a name only.

Caradoc said, "You are certain?"

"I am sure as to my facts. But as you pointed out, there can be no such thing as certainty." Bochner was enjoying his triumph. "I tracked him, do you understand? I followed his trail. From the site to the town, to where he went to find help, to where he gained it, to where he went to find another."

"So easily?"

"He was on the move and relying on speed more than covering his trail. He knew he couldn't do that. There had been a fight and he had killed a man. After that he had to run." His laughter rose. "To here, Cyber. To this town. To a tavern close to the field. A week and we would have lost him. A couple of days, even, but I was hunting him down. Me, Cyber! Me!"

His pride was a beacon, a force which drove him to pace the room, to halt before the uncurtained window, to turn and pace again before the desk at which the cyber sat with poised immobility.

"So you have tracked him down," said Caradoc. "You know just where Dumarest is to be found. All that remains is to reach out and take him. Correct?"

"Not exactly."

"Explain." Caradoc listened then said, "The *Belzdek*—how can you be so sure?"

"The name the woman gave me. It was that of a captain. Jarge Krell. The *Belzdek* is his vessel."

"And you assume that Dumarest must be on it?" As Bochner nodded the cyber added, "But, of course, the woman could have lied."

"No!"

"What makes you so certain? Have you yet to learn that nothing is ever certain? How can you be convinced she did not lie? After all, you could hardly have been regarded by her as a friend."

Tortured, dying—no, she would not have considered him that.

Caradoc said, "Assuming that Dumarest killed Menser, we have a time node from which to base extrapolations. If he left the site immediately, he would have arrived in the town by sunset. Allow more for him to have met the woman and be treated by her, more still for him to have gone to any rendezvous she might have arranged."

"To meet Krell."

"He or another. What is of more concern is the ship departures during the relevant period." Caradoc picked a paper from a sheaf on his desk. "Five vessels left in the period between Menser's death and our arrival; the *Belzdek*, *Frome*, *Entil*, *Wilke* and *Ychale*. The latter is an ore-carrier plying between Ealius and Cham on a regular schedule. The *Wilke* is a vessel of a commercial line operating a circular route and touching at Ninik, Pontia, Vult and Swenna. The others are traders going where the dictates of cargo and passengers take them." Caradoc lowered the paper. "Well?"

Bochner said, thoughtfully, "Dumarest didn't pass through the gate."

"He didn't subject himself to the lie detector at the gate," corrected the cyber. "Which means he either smuggled himself through or surmounted the perimeter fence. As that is watched and guarded by electronic devices, and as no alarm was recorded, it is safe to assume that he left Ealius by deception."

"And he had to leave," said Bochner. "An animal on the run can only think of finding a safe place in which to hide. Where, on this world, could Dumarest find that? After killing Menser, he would be marked for assassination by the man's friends. Certainly he would have become prominent, and that would be the last thing he wanted." He frowned, remembering the woman, her tormented eyes, the way she had spat before she had screamed out the name. Had she lied? Would she have retained sufficient resolve? "The *Belzdek*," he decided. "I say Dumarest is on the *Belzdek*."

"Which left for Gorion as we landed. The *Entil* left the previous noon for Vult. The *Frome* earlier for your own world of Pontia. Five vessels in all and the possibility remains that Dumarest could be on any one of them." Pausing, he ended, "Now tell me, hunter, how would you find your prey?"

"Set traps. Radio ahead and—" Bochner broke off, remembering. "No," he said bitterly, "it's not as easy as that. We're in the Rift. In the Quillian Sector. Damn it! Damn it all to hell!"

Chapter Four

Vult was as Allain had claimed: a mad world inhabited by the insane. In the sky the sun, huge, mottled with flaring patches of lemon and orange, burned with a relentless fury, and at night the stars glittered like a host of hungry, watching eyes. Stars which were close, suns which filled space with conflicting energies, radiations which disturbed the delicate neuron paths of the brain, dampening the censor so that between thought and action there was little restraint. A harshly savage world where only the strong could hope to survive.

"A bad place, and we've arrived at a bad time." Jumoke looked at the sky from where he stood, with Dumarest and Dilys at the head of the ramp. "Look at that sun! An electronic furnace scrambling the ether. There'll be murder and raping abroad. Be sure you're not the victims."

"Earl will see to that." The woman touched his arm. "Right, Earl?"

Her fingers lingered on the smooth plastic, a gesture the navigator chose to ignore if he saw it, but one Dumarest knew he would remember if he had. As if by accident he moved away from the caress, looking down over the field, the sagging fence around it, the cluster of people attracted by their arrival. One was on his way toward them.

"There's Inas," said Dilys. "I wonder what he'll have for us this time?"

Inas was the local agent, a Husai, his dark face adorned by the pattern of his beard. He touched Jumoke's palm, nodded to the woman, stared at Dumarest.

"Our replacement for Gresham," she explained. "Any news?"

"With the sun the way it is?" Inas lifted his eyebrows.

"You know better than that, my dear. We can hope for nothing until the activity dies and even then the messages will have to be decoded. You?"

"Nothing but static all the way." Jumoke stepped back and made way for the agent to enter the ship. "Anything good for us?"

"A party for Ellge. They wait in town. Interested?"

"We could be, if the price is right and nothing better turns up. Still, that's up to the captain. He's in the salon with a bottle. Wait a moment and I'll take you up." He turned to look at the others. "Remember what I said now, be careful."

A warning Dumarest intended to heed. Even as they crossed the field he could sense the invisible energies prickling his skin despite the protective mesh in his clothing, the gray plastic he had chosen to wear rather than his uniform. It was more comfortable, offered better protection and the knife in his boot was a sign most would recognize and be warned.

Dilys said, "How many worlds have you visited, Earl? I don't mean called at like this, but actually lived on for a while. A dozen? A score?" She turned her head to look at his face. "More than that?"

"I forget."

"You didn't keep count?" She saw him smile and realized she was talking like an impressionable child. Well, he had impressed her, damn him! "I suppose after the first dozen they all begin to look the same. Like women. Isn't that so, Earl? Isn't that what most men think?"

"I don't know what most men think, Dilys."

"You must have heard them talk. Boast, even. About all cats being grey at night. Men!"

He said mildly. "Are they like that? Men, I mean. Don't they all begin to act and sound and look alike after the first dozen or so?"

"How should I know?"

"You're a woman—"

"But not a whore!" Then, as she looked at him, her anger vanished and she smiled. "All right, Earl, you win. I should know better than to talk like that. In our game, we're all the same. Sex makes no difference; we work together, take the same risks and share the same rewards."

"You really believe that?"

"Of course. Why do you ask."

He moved on, not answering, wondering if she was being deliberately obtuse; if any woman with her degree of femininity could ever delude herself that she was regarded as other than what she was. If so, Jumoke could educate her; the man was obviously in love with her. A love which he seemed to contain, to hold in private, as if to expose it would be to destroy it. A weakness, perhaps, but some men were like that; fearing to lose all if they hoped to gain too much.

"Mister!" A man, young, barely more than a boy, came running toward them, his eyes on Dumarest. "You the handler on that ship? Can you give me passage? Please, mister, can I ride with you?"

"Where do you want to go?"

"Anywhere. Just as long as I get away from this place. Hell itself, if that's where you're going. It can't be worse than Vult."

Dilys said, "We can carry you if you've got the price. Have you?" She shook her head as he mentioned what he had. "It isn't enough for a High passage, but we could take you if you're willing to ride Low."

"No!" Dumarest was sharp. "No!"

"Why not?"

"You heard what I said." He took her arm and pushed her past the youngster, who stared after them with sunken, desperate eyes. "Don't argue with me. Not in public. Not before that boy."

She said nothing until he had led her into a tavern and had ordered drinks. They were tart, strong, arriving dewed with condensation and tinkling with ice.

Looking at her glass, Dilys said, "Why, Earl?"

"Why am I buying you a drink? Let's just say that I like you and want to be friends."

"I'm talking about that boy out there. You turned down a chance to make a profit. Why?"

He said flatly, "Carry that boy and you'd arrive with a corpse. He hasn't the fat on him to survive. He hasn't the strength. He's starved too long and worked too hard to get a stake and, if we take it from him, we'll be taking his life."

"A chance he's willing to take, Earl." She was stubborn. "A chance you've no right to stop him taking."

"Have you ever ridden Low?" The flicker of her eyes gave him the answer. "No. Have you ever opened a casket and seen someone lying dead? I thought not. You wouldn't like it if you did. You'd like it a lot less if you knew, when you put him into the box, that you were putting him into a coffin. Believe me, girl, I'm trying to save that boy's life."

She stared at him, her eyes searching, then she said slowly, "Yes, I really believe you mean that. You care about that boy. But why, Earl? What is he to you? What does it matter if he should die while we carry him?" Then, understanding, she added, "You. You're thinking of yourself when young. When you were like that boy, perhaps; young and scared and a little desperate. Did someone save you then? Is that it? Are you repaying an old debt?"

He said bluntly, "I was lucky."

With a luck which was still with him. No message could have been received on Vult from Ealius. If the Cyclan were on his trail, they were still one step behind—a distance he hoped to increase.

"Earl?" The woman was watching him, her eyes lambent, understanding. "Earl, you—"

He said, "Drink up and let's get about your business. We don't want Jumoke to get worried."

They had come to shop, which was Allain's work, but he refused to set foot on the world he had reason to hate, and Dilys had volunteered to replenish the ship's store of luxury items and what staples were needed. Dumarest followed her from the tavern into the commercial complex, where thick roofs of translucent crystal softened the glare of the sun, and inset panels of variegated colors threw a multihued swath of rainbow brilliance over the covered walks and promenades, the fronts of shops, the seats on which people lounged, their eyes ever-watchful.

They wore colors as bright as their sun; blouses and tunics set and studded with odd shapes of metal, stones, scraps of quartz, minerals which glowed like fireflies—fabrics either dull or shimmering with chemical sheens, winks and glitters and somber patches. They could have been clowns, but no clown came armed with spines and spikes on shoulders and joints, carried knives and clubs at their belts, sported tomahawks, cutlasses, cleavers, helmets set with slitted visors, trailing plumes. A populace armed and armored, touchily aggressive, watchful and radiating a feral zest.

If nothing else those inhabiting Vult were strongly alive.

Dilys sensed the atmosphere and responded to it as she walked close at Dumarest's side. Colors seemed to grow brighter, the pulse of blood through her veins, stronger, the air itself held a sharp and virile fragrance. The scent of violence, she thought, if violence could be said to have an odor of its own. The scent of physical bodies tense and aware of the possibility of combat. The exudation of people who had to be constantly on their guard, constantly alert.

"Earl!" A man had screamed from an adjoining way, and another had cursed as if with anger rather than pain. A flurry, and they were past the opening, Dumarest not altering his stride, doing no more than glancing down the path dimmed and shadowed with dusty purple light. "Earl, someone is—"

"We mind our own business. Is this the place?"

The store had thick windows meshed with strips of metal, doors which were held fast with electronic devices, a floor which glowed with warning light, displays in which goods could be seen but not touched.

Assistants who were armed.

"Madam, sir, it is my pleasure to serve you!" The man wore a quilted jacket and pants puffed and bright with metal. The helmet winked with polished gems and, as Dumarest lifted his hand, the visor fell to mask the face, the eyes.

"My apologies." A hand lifted the metal screen back into place. "A misunderstanding. The movement of your hand— I'm sure you understand."

A hand which could have been fitted with a container of acid. A movement which could have sent it into the eyes.

"Your needs?"

Dilys produced a list and read off items, frowning at the prices quoted, altering, taking alternatives which, the man assured her, were every bit as good.

"If they aren't, I'll be back," she warned. "And if I find cause for complaint, you'll lose more than our trade."

"If you are dissatisfied, then full compensation will be made. And for you, sir? Is there any item which arouses your interest? You are a visitor, I know, but it would be prudent to display arms. A short sword, or a small axe balanced for throwing? A club, or at least a whip which can be worn at the wrist?"

And one which would stir the aggressive natures of all who saw it, inviting challenges and combats and bloody meetings.

Dumarest said, "Have you a gun?"

"A gun?" The man blinked. "Certainly, sir, but are you sure of what you are asking? Had you been carrying one, the charges would have detonated as you entered this store. Had it been a laser, the energy cell would have vented its potential in the form of heat. Outside, on the streets, in taverns, well—you understand?"

A temptation to any who saw the weapon. A greater challenge than a whip and a greater prize. One they would not hesitate to kill to obtain, or kill to prevent being used, or use to prevent others similarly armed from killing. To carry a gun openly displayed on Vult was to invite destruction. To use one, the same. Only in houses could such protection be safely owned.

"I take the liberty of mentioning this because you are strangers," said the man. "But should you want a gun, we can supply it. Delivered, of course, and under guard. Now, if you will tell me the type and caliber, any decoration you may desire, any adaptation?"

"Never mind." Dumarest turned to the woman. "Have you finished?"

"Here, yes, but I need some abrasive compounds. From Hartleman?"

"Yes, madam, as you say." The man nodded agreement to the question. "I shall call ahead to warn him of your arrival."

Hartleman was bored, pleased for the company, eager to talk of worlds he had known as a boy, of Vult, to which he had come a score of years earlier. He served barley water tisane and small cakes, and bemoaned his lot at the same time as he praised his wares and reputation. Trade was good, but trade could be better. Violence was bad, but he had known it worse. The radiation was on the increase, but the scientists said that it could be followed by a period of comparative calm. And, yes, he could deliver the abrasives to the field for a small extra charge, but his son was nursing a wound and his daughter, well, who would allow a girl to wander without an escort on Vult? His eyes studied the woman.

"How large is the parcel?" said Dumarest. He nodded at the answer. "We'll carry it."

It was small but heavy, pastes of diamond-hard fragments and others of fine emery, powders which flowed like water and grits, and scored the fingers if touched. Packed in two bundles, connected by a strap, they made a drag on his shoulder.

"Ready?" Dumarest waited as the woman made effusive farewells. Impatience edged his voice. Why was she taking so long? "Come on, now. Let's move!"

She fell into step beside him, containing her own irritation, knowing it, and his impatience, to be the result of the radiation streaming from the setting sun. The light in the promenades had dulled, somber shadows lying where once had blazed lemons and ambers, violets, blues, greens and purples. Dusky areas where gold and silver had cast shimmering pools.

Shadows in which creatures stirred and came to life with fading glimmers from bizarre adornments.

"Earl!"

"Keep walking."

There were five of them, edging close, eyes moving like restless insects beneath the rims of helmets, hands twitching at belts, weapons, clothing. Young men with hard faces, and mouths containing teeth filed and extended to give them the appearance of wolves.

Scavengers.

Hunters with brains tormented by the disturbing radiation.

Madmen after fun.

Two halted down the promenade as two others moved to stand, one at each side, the fifth taking up the rear. Those ahead blocked progress, waiting as Dilys slowed, stepping forward as she halted to run curved hands over the prominences of her breasts.

"Nice," said one. "Good meat, eh, Felix?"

"Good legs." His companion had a cheek ravaged with scars, eyes enhanced with flaring tattoos. "Long and solid and smooth all over. I bet she could crack a man's ribs if she had a mind. Crush him to a pulp—a fine way to go, right, Val?"

"You said it," said the man on the right. "You said it."

"Big," said the man on the left. "Like a mountain. I've never had a woman like that. She's big enough to get lost in. Big enough to handle us all at the same time. Give us a lot of fun. What say, Cia?"

The man at the rear had a voice which dripped like turgid oil.

"I say we waste time. Let's see what's under the wrappings."

Cloth ripped, as the man standing at the woman's side tore at her blouse. Flesh showed, smooth, golden, the expanse widening as the fabric yielded, the twin mounds of her breasts showing to attract all eyes.

The moment for which Dumarest had been waiting.

He spun, hand lifted, fingers stiff, stabbing like blunted spears at the throat of the man behind. A blow which ruptured delicate tissues, numbed vital nerves, sent the man to the ground, twitching, gasping, blood spreading from his mouth. As he dropped, Dumarest continued the turn, foot lifting, boot lashing out to slam against the man at his side, to send him staggering back, doubled, vomiting from the agony of crushed testicles.

"Felix!"

The man with the tattooed eyes was already in action. He was fast, smooth, metal glinting as he clawed at his belt and lifted a knife. The man at his side dragged a cutlass from its sheath. Val, the man at the woman's side, jumped back like a spider to stand hunched, a small axe in each hand.

"Bastard," he said. "You hurt. Bastard!"

"We'll get him," said Felix. "We'll have him down and take his eyes, his ears, the tongue out of his mouth, the meat from between his legs. Then we'll see about what to do with the woman—Val!"

Dumarest sprang backwards as the man lunged forward, axes gleaming. Dilys screamed as a razor edge touched her hair and sent a golden strand falling to her shoulder, screamed again as blood showed in a thin, red line across her chest; screams intended to distract, to divert. echoing high and shrill as Dumarest backed, dropping the strap from his shoulder, the band weighed at each end with the abrasive pastes. Air whined as he whirled it in a tight circle, released it, sent it wheeling through the air to hit an upraised arm, to wrap around it, to slam against the face behind the fragile protection.

Dilys grabbed one of the axes as the man fell, lifted it, swung it hard against the exposed jaw, the flat side making a dull, liquid sound as it shattered bone.

"Get them!"

Her attack had been a mistake, one she recognized as Felix shouted. She should have moved away and remained mobile, instead she was now stooping over the man she had struck, awkwardly placed, an easy victim for the man who came running toward her with his cutlass lifted high. A matter of moments. Dumarest could handle either, but not both at the same time. But he was on his feet and had the better chance.

As Felix ran toward him, Dumarest dropped his hand, lifted it weighted with the knife he'd snatched from his boot, swung it back and forward to send the blade lancing through the air in a calculated throw. As it landed, the man with the tattooed eyes drove his own knife hard into Dumarest's stomach.

A gamble taken and won—had the man aimed for the throat or face, the steel would have done its work. As it was, the point ripped into the plastic then glanced upwards as it struck the metal buried beneath. A blow which hit like the kick of a horse, but one Dumarest gave the man no chance to repeat. His hand fell, gripped the knife-wrist, squeezed and twisted and his other hand darted forward, the fingers closing around the throat, digging into the tissue to impact against the carotids, stilling the flow of blood to the brain and bringing immediate unconsciousness. A pressure which, if maintained, would bring death.

Dropping the limp figure, Dumarest said, "Dilys?"

She was standing beside the fallen body of the man who had carried the cutlass, blood making a scarlet swath over her exposed flesh, breasts rising and falling as they betrayed her agitation.

"Animals," she said. "Beasts. They would have killed you and—"

"They could have friends." Dumarest knelt and jerked his knife free from the dead man's spine, wiping the blade before thrusting it back into his boot. Slinging the abrasives over his shoulder, he said, "Cover up and let's get out of here."

The party for Ellge arrived at dusk and with them bales and crates and the artifacts constructed of ironstone and silicates found in the deserts of Vult; things found by the party which consisted of archaeologists delving for evidence of a race which could have preceded the present inhabitants. One which was suspected to be other than human.

"Men, as we know them, must have been a fairly recent development," said Aares Atanya with dry precision. "An influx from some overpopulated world, or a colony choosing Vult on which to establish their own form of society. Such things are common. But I am certain that before they arrived there was another viable culture which had adapted itself to local conditions. A life form which could have evolved here, if not introduced by the same means as the present inhabitants. Some of the items we found could not have been used by mankind. Their shape is unsuited to the human hand, and yet they are undoubtedly tools. The conclusions are interesting, and further evidence could show traces of movements which could upset all our accepted beliefs as to our own origins."

"Because Vult may, at one time, have supported a race of lizards or toads?" One of the others, a young girl with heavily lidded eyes, smiled as she looked at Dumarest. "You mustn't get carried away, Aares."

"And you must learn to have a more open mind, Gliss."

"But not too open." The younger man sitting beside her closed his hand protectively on her own. "We must adhere to the principle of scientific investigation and logical truth. For example, I've heard people say that all life must have originated on one planet. An obvious absurdity—how could one small world have supported all the variegated types we know? If life had evolved on a single planet, then surely all men would look the same? As it is, we have skins ranging in color from alabaster to the deepest ebony, hair from silver to jet, eye color, shape of skulls, subtle differences of limbs—" The man shrugged. "Even to think of all men having a common origin is patently absurd."

Dumarest said, "But isn't there evidence to support such a supposition? We all belong to the same species, surely? If not, how could we interbreed?"

"The same species, yes," admitted the man, "but only if you accept the ability to interbreed as a sign of similarity. That could be quite accidental. My own feelings are that life evolved on worlds of similar type and so would have evolved on similar lines."

"You're forgetting the basic chemical composition," said

another. "The blueprint of the DNA units surely proves that for all mankind there has to be a common point of origin. I don't mean all came from a single world. As you say, that is ridiculous, but what if we were 'planted'. By that, I mean supposing that, long ago in the past, a superior race passed through this galaxy and seeded suitable worlds with specialized compounds. Spores or sperm or seeds which became life as we know it? That would account for the diversity of types found on a variety of worlds, and also the fact we can interbreed."

Gliss said firmly, "That's fantasy, Ulk, and you know it."

"Speculation, my dear. Of course, if you'd rather believe in accident, or the idiocy of a single common origin on a small, lonely world, that's your privilege. Or perhaps you have a more esoteric belief? A superior being, for example, one who—"

Dumarest said dryly, "I thought that was your belief. A superior race, a superior being—surely they are the same?" Then, as the girl shot him a grateful look, he added, "Would anyone care to join me in a game?"

It was going to be a poor trip, he decided when later he retired to his cabin. The archaeologists had preferred to talk rather than gamble, and while their conversation held interest, it wouldn't swell the profits. Only the girl, Gliss, had shown interest and Dumarest was certain that it wasn't in games of chance.

He rose when, an hour after he had lain down, the door clicked open to reveal a figure standing in the opening. The girl, he was sure, and hoped he could handle her without too much fuss. Then she spoke and he realized his mistake.

"Earl?"

"Dilys—is something wrong?"

"No." Clothing rustled as she stepped into the cabin and closed the door behind her. In the darkenss, she said, "I wanted—that is—Earl, I haven't had a chance to thank you for what you did."

"Forget it."

"I can't."

"Why not? We're shipmates, aren't we? We're supposed to help each other. You would have done the same."

"No, Earl, I couldn't. The way you moved, your speed, that knife you threw. If it hadn't been for you, those men—"

He said quickly, "Forget it. It's over. You owe me nothing."

"I disagree, Earl. May I talk?"

"If you want." Fully awake now, he remembered something. "How did you open my door?"

"With the master key." She paused as if awaiting his objection and when none came she said, "How was it in the salon?"

"Slow. We'll get little extra this trip."

"From the men, no, but from the women?" Her voice held a question. "I saw the way they looked at you. That young one in particular. Gliss, I think her name is. Gliss. She was lingering in the passage when I came along and I was surprised to find your door locked."

"If it hadn't been, would you have entered?"

"I—"

"If I'd been entertaining, then the door would have been locked," he reminded. "What would you have done had I not been alone?"

"Broken the bitch's neck!" Then, while he was still assessing the intensity of her answer, she added, "No, Earl, I don't mean that. Not really. I—damn it, why can't you help me? Why won't you understand?"

Something fell on his cheek, a touch of wetness followed by another. Rearing up on the bed, he felt for the panel, found it, touched a switch and caused moonglow to illuminate the darkness. In the pale luminescence he saw her face, her eyes, the tears which filled them to stream down her cheek.

"I love you," she said. "Earl, I love you."

"Jumoke?"

"Thinks I'm his property. We've been lovers, yes, but he doesn't own me. No man does that. Not now or ever. Not even you, Earl, though I'd walk barefoot over broken glass to be at your side. But you don't own me. No man can ever do that."

She was protesting too strongly, rejecting something he hadn't offered, defensive when there was no need. A woman too sensitive about her size, perhaps; one who must have suffered the scorn of others when young. Finding a haven on the ship and doing work which made her the equal of any. An environment in which she didn't have to meet opposition or face the competition of her own sex. Or perhaps it was more than simply a matter of size. A secret vulnerability which robbed her of the strength needed in order to survive in hostile situations. He remembered the recent attack, the way she had frozen, to act the way she had, in a fury of misguided and unnecessary effort. The man she had hit had already been rendered harmless. The effort used to smash his jaw had been an act that had endangered her life.

"Earl?"

"I'm thinking.".

"Of us?"

Of Jumoke, and the expression he'd seen in the navigator's eyes on their return to the ship. Of the way the man had watched Dilys. His hurt when she had turned from him. His pain when she had praised what Dumarest had done.

"It's normal," she said quietly. "Ship-marriage, I mean. To last as long as either of us wants it to. No obligations."

"I know."

"You've had one before?"

"Yes." He looked at her and, in the moonglow, saw Lallia with her mane of ebon hair. Lallia, now long dead and long since dust. "Yes," he said again. "I've been ship-wed. But not again. Not with you."

"Am I so repulsive?"

"No." How could he explain? How to tell a woman in love that her love was not returned? How to be kind when he was being cruel? "Listen," he said, "and try to understand. You are a lovely woman and an intelligent one. Too intelligent to act the child and cry when you can't get your own way. And I think too much of you to lie. I like you, yes, but I don't want to marry you. Not even ship-marry you. I—"

He broke off as she rested her fingers against his lips. They were soft and held the scent of perfume, a heady fragrance which strengthened as she leaned forward to look into his eyes.

"No," she whispered. "Say no more. I understand. You are trying to save me from hurt, but when has pleasure ever been free of pain? You are kind, Earl, and gentle. And you care. My darling, you care!"

Chapter Five

On Ellge, they picked up a dancer, a woman of fading beauty with a heavily painted face, hands which held the likeness of claws, eyes the bleakness of glass. A creature long past her prime, now moving to worlds of lesser competition. Those with a cruder appreciation of her art, on which she could still earn a living and, perhaps, find a man to support her to the end of her days.

On Vhenga, they took on a dispenser of charms; a thin-faced man with an embroidered cloak and a box filled with strange nostrums and exotic ointments. The dancer stayed on, finding a kindred soul in the seller of charms, spending long hours huddled with him over the gaming table in the salon, where she played her cards as if they were pieces of her own flesh.

On Cheen, they were joined by two dour engineers, a time-served contract man from the mines and a minor historian from the Institute.

On Varge, they took on a professional dealer in items of death.

Like the dispenser of charms, he was tall, thin-faced, sparse in body, but where Fele Roster had crinkles in the corners of his eyes and a wry smile wreathing his lips, thin though they might be, Shan Threnond's face was a mask from which he looked with cynical indifference on a universe he had taken no part in making, and which he understood all too well.

A man of business, who wasted no time in setting up his trade in the salon, unwilling to waste a moment as the *Entil* hurtled through the void, wrapped in the humming, space-eating power of its Erhaft drive.

"Here we have a small item which must hold interest for all who value the safety of their skins," he murmured as, with deft hands, he set out his wares on the rich darkness of a velvet cloth. "In the shape of a ring, as you see, and the stone and mounting are of intrinsic value. But note, the stone is drilled and contains three darts, each of which can be fired by a simple contraction of the muscle. The stone can be removed and recharged so as to allow practice. Observe." He slipped the ring on a finger, aimed it at a scrap of board, lowered the appendage at the second joint. Those watching heard a barely audible *spat* and, on the board, a thing shrilled with vicious life. Almost immediately, it created an area of disintegration around it; a pit which dribbled a fine dust and from which, finally, it fell.

"The harmonics are destructive to all organic matter," said the dealer quietly. "The area affected is half as deep as it is wide. In flesh there are toxic side effects. The shock-impact is vast, the pain is great and, aimed at the throat, death is certain."

"Unless the dart is quickly removed?"

"Yes." Shan Threnond glanced at the dancer. "You know of these things, madam?"

She ignored the stilted courtesy. "I've seen them before. And, on Heldha, I saw a man whipped to the edge of death for owning such a thing."

"A backward world, my lady."

"A logical one." One of the engineers rasped a hand over his chin. "They don't like assassins."

"Does anyone?" Threnond lifted his shoulders in a shrug. "But a man must protect himself. Surely you would not deny anyone that right? And a woman must take elementary precautions against those who would do her harm. You, my lady, must have had experience of such dangers. At least, felt at times the need to reduce the pressure of an unwanted passion, shall we say? This will do exactly that." He lifted another item from his store. "A ring again—but what better place to carry a weapon than on a finger? There it can remain, always in clear view, apparently harmless, yet ready for immediate action should the need arise. This contains a pressurized drug which can be blasted into a face. Within two seconds, the recipient will be stunned and helpless long

enough for the user to escape, change the situation, or summon aid."

"A whore's device." Fele Roster shook his head in distaste.
"No decent woman would ever allow herself to become involved in the kind of situation you mention."

"You talk like a fool," snapped the dancer. "Decency has
nothing to do with it. How much?"

"For the ring? In gold, with a genuine ruby, three hundred
urus. With a synthetic gem, a hundred less. For paste and
gilt, a hundred—the cost of the inner mechanism and charge
must, of course, remain the same."

"I'll take a synthetic." The dancer pointed with a hooked
finger. "That one. And another with the darts. How much for
both?"

Later, lying beside him in the snug confines of his cabin,
Dilys said, "Why did she buy such things, Earl? An old
woman like that."

"She is afraid."

"And so arms herself? Against what?"

Against the terrors of the mind, which were often more
frightening than those of reality. Against age itself, and imagined hunger. Against potential illness and poverty and
neglect. Against threats she had known and dangers she had
passed and could meet again. Like the scum they had met on
Vult, and others who haunted the dark corners of primitive
worlds.

Dilys said, after he'd explained, "Those rings won't give
her much protection if she is attacked. She could miss, or the
attacker could be armored, or there could be more than one.
And the mere attempt to defend herself could anger them."

"So?"

She flushed, grasping his meaning, sensing his lack of sym-
pathy with any who thought that way, or who imagined trouble could be avoided by the closing of eyes.

"Do you think I'm a coward, Earl?"

"No."

"But—?" She broke off as if waiting for an answer, and
when none came, continued, "It's my size. Just because
you're big, people think you must be hard and tough and aggressive, but it isn't like that at all. At least, not as far as I'm
concerned. I hate violence, and always have. When I see it, I
want to run away from it, and when I get mixed up in it, like

on Vult, I—well, I just can't handle it. If that isn't being a coward, what is?"

"I don't know."

"Don't lie to me, Earl."

"I'm not." Dumarest turned to look at her in the soft, nacreous lighting. Moonglow touched her cheeks and shadowed her eyes, glimmered from the rich, full contours of her naked body, touched breasts and hips and the curve of thighs with creamy halations. "Cowardice is determined by other people on the basis of what they think someone else should have done in a particular situation. It's also a cheap term of abuse. What we're really talking about is survival. Sometimes, in order to survive, you have to kill. At other times, you have to run. If you try to kill and fail, then you aren't brave, you're dead. If you run and escape, you aren't a coward, you're alive."

"Black and white," she said. "You make it sound all so simple. Either a thing is or it isn't, but surely there are shades of gray? Possibilities in between?"

"A man is either alive or dead," said Dumarest. "How can there be degrees between? He can be crippled or ill or diseased, but those are degrees of efficiency, not of life. He is alive until he is dead."

"And to stay alive, sometimes he has to run." She turned her head to look at him, the helmet of hair catching and reflecting the light to make a golden haze framing the broad planes of her face. "Have you ever had to run, my darling?"

"Yes."

"From home?" She repeated the question wanting, womanlike, to know of his early days. "Did you run away from home in order to seek adventure?"

"To avoid starvation," he said bluntly. "I was little more than a boy and I stowed away on a ship. I was more than lucky—the captain could have evicted me. Instead, he allowed me to earn my passage. A long time ago, now. A long time."

Long enough to have moved deeper into the galaxy where suns glowed hot and close, and shipping was plentiful. Into a region where even the very name of Earth had become the subject of humor. A planet forgotten, but one which he had to find. Would find.

"Home," she said gently. "Earth is your home and you

want to return. But why, Earl? If there was nothing for you there when you left, what can be waiting for you now?"

"Nothing."

"But—"

"You said it, Dilys. Home. A man can have only one."

A place to call his own. A world on which to settle and on which to make his mark. To build a house and raise a family, to find happiness and contentment. A dream, one born during the long, lonely journeys between the stars. An ideal nurtured to give a meaning to life, a reason for existing. A determination which drove him to find his world or die trying.

A waste! God, such a waste!

She felt his warmth close beside her, the comfort he gave, the sense of security she enjoyed when she was with him. A man of whom any woman could be proud. As she was proud when watching him at work in the salon, gambling with calm efficiency, apparently unaware of the stares thrown at him by women, the calculating appraisal of their eyes.

Could they sense the loneliness she had recognized? The bleak isolation in which he lived, the cold emptiness of life spent journeying from world to world, the frustration of an endless, hopeless search? And always a stranger among strangers, any liaison only temporary, any love doomed to wither, to fade, to die.

"Earl," she whispered, "don't you ever get tired? Don't you ever want to stop and settle down and live as most men do?" A question she waited in vain for him to answer. "I've some property on Swenna. It isn't much, a farm and enough ground to keep a dozen alive, but there is a river and the mountains are close and, at night during summer, the air is so sweet with perfume it can make you drunk. If you ever get tired, Earl, if you ever want a place to stay and rest and maybe relax awhile, it's yours. I'd be there, if you wanted me. And you wouldn't regret it, I swear to that." Her hand reached out to touch him, to glide in a possessive caress over his shoulder, his arm. "Think about it, darling. At least think about it."

In the shadows, something moved, a click and a portion of the chamber bloomed with variegated lights, the hologram seeming to hang suspended in the air, to have brought a literal section of space itself into the confined boundaries of the room.

"The Rift," said the technician. "As you ordered, my lord."

Caradoc said, "You are mistaken. I asked for a detailed display of the Quillian Sector."

"I—my apologies. A mistake. It will be corrected immediately."

And would never be repeated. A word, and the technician would be demoted, branded as an indifferent worker, denied accesss to the sophisticated equipment housed in the building of the Hafal-Glych—a slur on his reputation which he would never live down. And the word would be given. Cyber Caradoc had no time for carelessness and no patience where inefficiency was concerned. Now, as the display changed, he nodded and gestured dismissal. Only when alone did he step toward the shimmering profusion of multicolored lights and smoky blotches of roiling ebon which constituted the Quillian Sector.

A region of space overcrowded with suns, over-profuse with worlds, hyperactive with electronic forces. Energies which nullified the normal use of radio—even the high-beam transmitters operating at maximum power and negating the limitations of light were, at the best, erratic. An irritation and a danger, but steps had been taken and all was proceeding according to plan.

Soon, now, the man would be taken.

Soon, now, the long chase would be over and Dumarest would be held by the Cyclan to yield the secret he possessed and which they rightfully owned.

A step, and lights reflected their images on the taut features and the scarlet robe, little dots of blue and green, yellow and amber, violet and ruby—the latter lost against the fabric but showing like sores against the skin of Caradoc's face. A good analogy; the ruby points were planets on which humanoid life was impossible; worlds of reeking vapors, tormented volcanoes, boiling, acid seas, poisonous atmospheres.

The dots of other colors showed worlds and suns in various stages of development and activity.

The ebon blotches were the dust clouds which held the Quillian Sector as though in the palm of a close-cupped hand.

"Master." An acolyte had entered the room on silent feet. "A message from Edhal. The *Belzdek* reports negative."

So the woman had lied. Caradoc was not surprised; he had expected nothing less. Bochner could have been mistaken, or could have lied in turn for some devious reason of his own. A matter of small probability, but even though small, it existed and had to be taken into account. As all things had to be taken into account, each given a measure of relative importance and relevance, each set against all other available facts in order to arrive at an extrapolated prediction.

An exercise of a mind chosen and trained by the Cyclan, which judged intellectual ability to be prized above all else.

Again, Caradoc studied the glimmering display, mind active as he assessed various probabilities, traced various paths between the stars. Only when he had exhausted all applicable combinations did he step back and head toward the door leading to the small private room placed at his disposal by those who ran the Hafal-Glych for the combine's true owners.

"Total seal," said Caradoc. "I am not to be disturbed for any reason."

"Master." The acolyte bowed and moved to take up his position outside the door. His life would be spent in guarding it, should the need arise.

Within the room, Caradoc touched the wide bracelet banding his left wrist. Invisible energy streamed from it, creating a zone of force through which no electronic eye or ear could operate. An added precaution to ensure his absolute privacy, as was the curtained window and the locked and guarded door.

Taking his place on a narrow cot, Caradoc closed his eyes and concentrated on the Samatchazi formulae. Gradually, his senses blurred and lost their function. Had he opened his eyes he would have been blind. Isolated in the prison of his skull, his mind ceased to be irritated by external stimuli and by means of the self-induced sensory deprivation, became a thing of pure intellect; its reasoning awareness the only conscious link with life. Only then did the engrafted Homochon elements become roused from quiescence. Rapport was soon established.

Caradoc took on a new dimension of life.

It was as if his mind had expanded to become a shimmering bubble which drifted among a host of other bubbles, all resplendent in variegated colors. A universe filled with glowing beauty which merged and wended one against the other to swirl and adopt new and ever-changing patterns of mathematical symmetry. Light which burned away the darkness of ignorance. Colors which expanded the visual spectrum. Form which held content. Content which held truth. Truth fashioned in a web which spanned the universe of which he was a living, active part. A part even as, at the same time, he was the whole. A bubble among other bubbles which were one bubble reflected to infinity.

At the heart of the shimmering beauty, at the very epicenter of the shifting patterns, rested the headquarters of the Cyclan. Buried far beneath the surface of a remote world, the central intelligence absorbed his knowledge as a desert absorbs water. A mental communication of almost instantaneous transference against which mechanical means of supralight contact were the merest crawl.

A moment, and then it was over.

The rest was sheer enjoyment, a mental intoxication which flooded his being and filled his brain with dancing motes of euphoric delight. Always was this period after rapport during which the Homochon elements sank back into quiescence and the machinery of his body began to realign itself with mental harmony. Caradoc floated in an ebon nothingness while he experienced strange, unlived situations, scraps of memory, fragments of exotic experiences, memories filled with outré images—the residue of other intelligences, the overflow of other minds.

It came from the aura surrounding the tremendous installation of central intelligence, the radiated power of the great cybernetic complex which was the heart of the Cyclan. One day, he would be a part of that installation. His body would age and fail but his brain would be saved, removed from his skull and joined in series with the millions of other brains taken from cybers who had lived before him and now continued to live as disembodied brains in vats of nutrient fluid. He would live as they lived, totally divorced from the irking irritations of the body, able to concentrate on matters of pure thought. A time of endless tranquillity in which he and they would work to solve each and every problem of the galaxy.

The reward of every cyber, but one which would be denied to him should he fail.

Opening his eyes, Caradoc stared at the ceiling, waiting for his motor functions to reach optimum before rising from the couch. A touch, and the bracelet was deactivated. The acolyte bowed as he left the room˷and entered the chamber to stand once again before the display.

"Master?"

The acolyte was bold, but Caradoc could appreciate his interest. And no potential cyber could be other than proudly alert—a trait to be encouraged as long as that pride did not usurp respect.

He said, "Verification of the report from the *Belzdek*. Negative as stated. The *Wilke* and the *Ychale* have been eliminated." Reports from cybers fed through central intelligence and passed on directly to his brain. Another report which he did not mention and an urgency about which he would think later.

"Which leaves the *Entil* and the *Frome*, master."

"Both traders and both operating in the Quillian Sector." Caradoc looked at the acolyte. It was never too soon to test the desired ability, and never a mistake to encourage its development. Practice in extrapolation, as in so many other things, led to perfection. "Your conclusions?"

For a moment the youth hesitated, then made his decision. "The *Entil* master."

A guess? If so, the habit must be eliminated. If not, the steps leading to the deduction could be elucidated.

"Explain."

"Both vessels are traders, master, but the *Frome* headed initially for Pontia. From there, it would be logical for it to make for Ninik, and then on to Swenna."

"Why?"

"The relative values of available cargoes. Pontia is a producer of leathers, oils, furs and feathers, articles of bone, concentrates of glandular excretions. There is a market for such things on Ninik. There, a cargo of tools and electronic components could be bought for sale on Swenna."

"Which is mostly an agricultural world." Caradoc nodded. The reasoning had been sound, but it betrayed a simplistic grasp of the essential elements of the situation. "And from Swenna, the *Frome* would have headed outward to the edge of the Quillian Sector? Correct?"

"Yes, master."

"Unless, of course, a cargo of high value was offered for immediate transport to a different world than those which you mentioned. Or a group of passengers bought a charter. Or the captain, because of some intuition, made a diversion. Or a local electronic storm forced the navigator to change course." Or that Dumarest, and the luck riding with him, had, by his mere presence, altered the natural sequence of logical events and introduced a "wild" factor, as he seemed to have done so often before; a thing Caradoc didn't mention. Instead he continued, "You appreciate how the most obvious pattern can be distorted by the smallest of unexpected events. Such events must always be included in any prediction you may make. In this case, however, you are correct. Dumarest is not on the *Frome*."

And had never been on it—a fact he had gained from his recent contact with central intelligence. Which meant that unless he had left the vessel, Dumarest must still be on the *Entil*.

Caradoc took a step closer to the shimmering display. Somewhere among the suns, the dots representing the ship would be moving, halting at worlds which he saw only as minute flecks of color. Short journeys, some taking only a few subjective hours. Short stopovers—no trader made a profit by hugging dirt. Destinations determined by the availability of cargoes or the needs of paying passengers. The ship moving in a pattern so erratic as to be almost purely random.

And, hunting it, Leo Bochner was intent on finding his prey.

He stood beneath a sky of maroon shot with clouds of umber, which shifted to burn with abrupt, coruscating brilliance catching the eye and filling the heavens with breathtaking splendor. Clouds made of millions of reflective particles which caught the rays of the rising sun and hurled them to all sides in sheets and blazes of luminous effulgence. A kaleidoscope of broken rainbows which would diminish as the day progressed and the dawn wind died, to return at sunset when again the winds would blow and the drifting mirrors would paint the firmament with poetry in light. An artist's dream and an awesome spectacle which, even now, was being recorded for the inhabitants of a mist-shrouded world a score of parsecs distant.

Bochner strolled to where Gale Andrel sat with her recording apparatus, her slim, lithe figure snug in form-fitting fabrics, the material delineating her petite femininity. A figure overwhelmed, it seemed, by the bulk of the apparatus which aimed wide lenses at the sky; an impression corrected by the deft motion of her slender hands as she adjusted verniers. The machine was the servant, and the woman its master, as she worked to balance scope and intensity. Too high a register in the lower end of the spectrum and the shimmering, ethereal loveliness of the violets would be dulled. Too much emphasis on the blues and the somber sullenness of the reds would lose their impact. Too high a level of brilliance would lessen fine detail and too dark an image would blunt sensory appreciation.

An attention to detail which had provided her with fame and wealth and an enviable reputation.

Bochner waited until she finally sighed and sat back in her chair, massaging her hands to ease the tension of tired muscles.

"Success, Gale?"

"Leo!" She smiled as she saw him. "Yes, I think so. Did you catch that interplay over the western horizon a few minutes ago? It was superb! That recording alone will sell at least a hundred thousand copies on Eltania."

"And on Phenge?"

"Phenge? No."

"A world of fog and misty shadows?"

"You'd think they'd snap up anything connected with light and beauty," she admitted. "I made that mistake five years ago—a recording of the ice waterfalls of Brell. The sun hits them at just the right angle twice a year, and if conditions are right, the result is fantastic. All the colors ever imagined mixed in the wildest profusion. It took me two years to get it just right, and when I did, I headed straight for Phenge. They weren't interested. They liked their mist and shadows and darkness and didn't want brightness and color. I doubt if I sold more than a score of recordings. Well, a girl learns."

"We all learn." Bochner glanced at the sky. "But some of us tend to forget. You've been out here since long before dawn and it's time you had something to eat. I've ordered a meal for the two of us and it's waiting for you to enjoy it. Ready?"

She hesitated, searching the sky, then rose from her chair and shrugged.

"You're right, Leo. I'll get nothing more until sunset. No!" She moved to prevent him lifting her equipment. "I'll manage."

A proud woman, he thought, as he followed her to the hotel. And a strong one. She carried the heavy apparatus with apparent ease. As he would carry his own if he was on a hunt, the pack on his back and the rifle at the ready, magazine loaded, sights adjusted, safety catch released—the mechanism an extension of himself as the missile it could hurl was an extension of his arm, his will.

To kill. To wait and savor the moment. To feel the godlike power cradled in his arms. To watch the target—the woman, for example. If he were about to shoot her, where would he aim? A few inches above the upper curve of her buttocks, he decided. The bullet sent to drive into the slight concavity at the base of her spine. To smash, to break, to shock, to kill. She would fall instantly, her head unmarked and suitable for mounting as a trophy.

He could visualize it set against its background of polished wood.

A small, round head, wreathed in a soft cloud of rich, brown hair. The eyes would stare from beneath slanting eyebrows, brown and sharply appraising, touched by a master hand to give them the semblance of life. The mouth would be slightly open to reveal the inner gleam of neat, white teeth, the lips themselves full and intriguing in their implied sensuality. The jut of the chin, with its shallow cleft. The slender column of the neck. The ears. The high forehead. The . . .

"Leo!" He blinked, instantly alert, as she called to him. "Daydreaming?"

"Thinking. Wondering how much longer we shall have to wait."

"It can't be long now." She set down her equipment and stretched as if unconscious of the way the gesture enhanced the firm thrust of her breasts. "Today, tomorrow, what does it matter?"

"It doesn't, if you're working." Bochner led the way to where a table stood beside a window, its surface loaded with glass and cutlery, china and covered dishes. As they sat, a waiter hurried forward to pour them both cups of fragrant tisane. "But what is there for me to do on Kumetat? If any game exists in the wilderness, it is small and relatively harmless. Suitable only for the training of beginners in the art of assessing the environment and location of the lair."

"And the stalk?"

He glanced at her and smiled. "The stalk! What can be better? The art of pitting your mind and strength, your skill and cunning, against another. A beast which would kill you if given the chance. A creature armed and armored by nature against which you are weak and defenseless aside from your own intelligence, the power of your mind."

"And, naturally, of your gun," she said dryly. "We must never forget the gun, must we?"

"You don't approve?"

"Of killing animals? No."

"Of hunting?"

"Of a stalk where, as you say, it is mind pitted against mind and cunning against cunning, yes. My father used to hunt when I was young and he took me with him when I was old enough to keep up. But he never carried a gun. He used a camera. It was enough to get up close and record the event. The fun, he used to say, was in the chase. The stalk. Any fool can kill."

He said blandly, "Of course. Now, may a fool offer you some refreshment? Slices of meat, cooked in a piquant sauce, and highly recommended by the chef? This compote of fruits, honey and nuts? A slice of bread coated with spiced seeds? An egg—they are worth trying. Or—" He broke off, looking at the hand she had placed on his own.

"Leo, I'm sorry."

"For calling me a fool?"

"You're not that, and we both know it. It's just that, well, a man with a gun never seems to give an animal a sporting chance. He stands back and fires and that's it, if he's any shot at all. Where's the danger?"

"For a man facing a beast which can't reach or hurt him—none," he admitted. "Such work is butchery. But to hunt a beast you must hit in exactly the right place with the single shot which is all time will allow, and first to track it to a point where it is at home and you are not—that isn't work for fools."

"Or for men?"

Too late, she tried to cover her distaste and, for a moment, he felt the anger rise within him; the burning rage which had always been his unconscious reaction to criticism and which, uncontrolled, could lead him to kill. Had led him to kill; the act itself a catharsis, easing as it cleansed—a luxury he could not at this time afford. Yet, it was hard to master his anger. That this mere recorder of transient spectacles should dare to deride him and what he represented! To mock the grim essentials of life itself! To ignore the fundamental truth which had accompanied mankind from the beginning and would stay with him until the end. How could she be such an ignorant fool?

And yet, looking at her as he reached for syrup and poured it over the chopped vegetables and prepared cereal in his bowl, he found it difficult to recognize her stupidity. Had the words been a mask? A test? A probe to trigger a reaction? Was she also, in her way, a hunter, and he her prey? Was she the bait skillfully offered to be withdrawn should he strike too fast or come too close?

Inwardly, he bared his teeth in a smile which was a tiger's snarl. If so, she had met her match. It was a game in which he did not lack experience.

He said, "Men do what they must. Some fight. Some hunt. Some kill. Always there must be those who hunt and those who are hunted. It is a law of nature."

"Yes," she said, and added in a peculiarly strained tone, "Life is a continuous act of violence."

"Of course. To live, it is necessary to kill." He gestured at the table, the plate of eggs, the dish of meat. The movement left no need for words. "We grow too serious. You record the beauty which you see and I, too, in a way, seek to provide a similar experience to those who are willing to pay for it. For death, in essence, is also beauty. As all great catastrophes are; fires, floods, volcanoes—"

"Destroyers," she said, musingly. "And I suppose the extinction of a personal universe could be regarded in such a light. After all, to the one involved, no catastrophe could be greater. The total erasure of all a living thing held to be real. An end. A termination." She shivered despite the warmth of the day. "Let's not talk about it."

A reluctance which did not match Bochner's assessment of her character. She was nothing if not strong, yet she had revealed a certain sensitivity he found interesting. Was it a mask to hide her real personality?

He remembered a predator on Rhius which spread false trails of pungent scent when pursued; exudations which contained subtle pheremones so that, entranced, those intent on the kill suddenly found themselves helpless victims to their imagined prey.

Was the girl such a one?

Did it matter if she was?

The afternoon, he decided, after she had bathed and changed and taken a little rest. When the sun had passed its zenith and the air still with sultry heat. She would be bored, restless, willing to indulge in a new experience. Intrigued by his attentions, and half-expecting him to call, as call he would. To sit in her room, her lair, to talk with her for awhile, to touch, to let the ancient magic work its biological charm and, even if she struggled, he would take her. He would make his symbolical kill.

But before the meal was over, the air quivered to the roar of manmade thunder as the *Entil* came in to land.

Chapter Six

The dancer still rode with them, as did the seller of nostrums and the dealer in items of death. The engineers had gone together with the time-served contract man, a scarred mercenary taking their place. Charl Zeda was a man who had lost a hard-won stake in a barren mine and was now headed back to richer worlds, whose rulers could afford the luxury of war.

Sitting beside the minor historian, he scowled at his cards. The game was poker and he did not play it well.

"Two," he said. "No, make it three."

A pair then, and he'd decided against holding a kicker. Dumarest dealt, watching as the man picked up the cards, noting the scarred face, the eyes, the hands. The face was a mask, the eyes blinded windows, but the hands betrayed him. He had not improved his hand.

"You?"

The historian took one. The dancer two. The dealer in death had passed, and so had Fele Roster. Gale Andrel had not joined the play.

Leo Bochner said, "I'll play these."

A bluff? It matched the impression Dumarest had of the man. He had not opened the bidding but that meant little—a man with a pat hand could have free choice. He had raised before the discards, a small sum which bought him the right to raise again if given the chance, but the others had merely called. Now he sat, his smooth face bland, his eyes a little amused, as if he were an adult pandering to children. A man killing time and unconcerned whether or not he won. A man who could be trying to buy the pot.

Dumarest glanced at it, then at his own hand. The three

lords he held should win if his calculations had been correct. The single card the historian had drawn showed he held two pairs, or had tried to fill a flush or complete a straight. From his reaction he had done neither nor had he matched either of his pairs. The dancer had played true to form, taking a wild chance and hoping for impossible odds to favor her hand. She could have gained similar cards to his own, but they would be weaker. Bochner was the unknown factor.

Dumarest watched him while appearing to study his cards. A hunter, now heading to worlds outside the Quillian Sector—the information he'd gained about the man had been small. His appearance told more; tall, smooth, his face bland, only the eyes gave a hint as to his nature. Eyes which were too steady, which held too long, as if the man were afraid ever to lessen his attention, as if he had long since learned that nothing was quite what it seemed. The eyes of a man who emitted a perpetual challenge—the holding of a stare until the other dropped his eyes.

And then?

Dumarest had met others with such a trait; fighters risking their lives in the arena with ten-inch naked blades. Men who had developed tricks in order to survive, who would hold a stare and maintain it until their opponents looked away, darting in as they did so, taking advantage of the movement to strike, to kill, to win.

But the man was a hunter, a friend of the woman, Gale Andrel, her lover, perhaps. It was natural that a hunter should have such eyes. Natural that he had the ability to sit as if made of stone. Natural that he should have been waiting on Kumetat?

The mercenary had opened. Now he thrust money into the pot. "Ten."

The historian hesitated, then threw in his hand. The dancer raised, light flashing from her gemmed hands as she doubled the bet. Bochner glanced at Dumarest.

"No limit?"

"None."

"Then I'll call and raise one hundred."

"You bastard!" Furious, the dancer threw down her cards. She had quit out of turn but no one objected. "Players like you ruin the game!"

Bochner ignored her. Ignored, too, the mercenary who had

dropped his cards to the baize and was obviously waiting to throw them in. "Well, Earl?"

On the face of it, a simple request as to whether Dumarest would call, raise or stack his hand, but meeting the cool appraisal of Bochner's eyes, he sensed it to be far more than that. Would he meet the challenge? Call the potential bluff? Face the enemy or run? Use his own skill and cunning to match that of his adversary? Was he willing to take a risk? Did he prefer always to be safe? Dared he admit the possibility of defeat?

Did he have courage? Did he have guts?

Dumarest checked the pot. Bochner's raise had almost doubled it which meant, allowing for what he'd put in earlier, he would be getting back over fifty per cent return on his money. A good investment for a few minutes work, and one favored by gamblers who saw a chance to use the weight of their money to buy the pot.

Dumarest said, "I'll call and raise another hundred."

A chance, but a calculated one, and it was time to discover the man's method of play. His hand could be stronger, but he had drawn only one card and Bochner could think he held less than he did. A single pair, even—a bluff took many forms.

"A hundred?" Bochner pursed his lips, one hand falling to toy with the coins before him, his eyes never leaving Dumarest's face. An old trick, to clink metal or rustle paper or allow chips to make their small drummings while watch was kept for the small, telltale signs of betrayal. The tension of the lips, the movements of the eyes, the impatience, the sweat, the very odor of a man under tension, of a man thirsting for the kill. "A hundred," he said again, this time not making it a question. Coins rose in his hand. "I think, in that case, I'll—well, I'll just give it to you."

"You quit?" The dancer grabbed at his cards. "What did you have?"

A blur and Bochner's hand was on her own, the fingers hard against her flesh, twisting so as to turn the ringed fingers down against the table.

"No," he said. "You don't see my cards. No one sees them."

"My wrist! You're hurting me!"

She rubbed at the bruised flesh as Bochner released her

hand then rose, fuming, to storm from the salon and into her cabin. Fele Roster rose and looked down at the others.

"I'd better follow her. There could be something I could do."

"Poison her," suggested the mercenary. "Some people live too long."

"She's no longer young, and worried, and not too well." The seller of nostrums backed from the table. "I've a compound which can bring her sleep and pleasant dreams. An illusion of youth which will not last, but will serve to ease her hurts. And you, sir," he glared at Bochner. "Perhaps you should remember that your mother was a woman and all women are worthy of a little consideration."

"A fool," said Charl Zeda, dispassionately, as the man left the salon. "He loves what was and now can never be. A woman long past her prime, with only the remnants of a once lovely body to commend her. Well, if you can't afford the cake, you can at least enjoy the crumbs."

"Fele is a romantic," said Shan Threnond. "He deals in charms and magic and has come to believe in the potency of an incantation. True, such things work with the yokels who come to gawk at his tricks at carnivals and fairs, but at such times, when does a love philter not work? A vial of colored water, a muttered spell, and nature will take care of the rest. It is much the same with his salves and lotions, his powders and pills and capsules, his compounds and nostrums. Chemicals mixed with herbs and natural oils which sting and smell and titivate and which, together with time, will either kill or cure."

"Unlike your own wares," said the historian dryly, "which only kill."

"Which protect," corrected the dealer. "Which are a precaution against a time of need." To Bochner, he said, "I noticed the way in which you twisted the woman's hand. Her rings?"

"I've seen rings like those before," said Bochner. "And I know how spiteful such a woman can be. There are those with faces marred by acid thrown by such as her. I wanted to keep mine intact."

"And your life and that of your lady?" Threnond glanced at Gale Andrel. "I must show you my wares. If nothing else, they will be of interest to a man like yourself, and the rings make appreciated gifts. Later, perhaps?"

"Later." Bochner looked at the cards. "Are we still playing?"

"You might be, I'm not." Charl Zeda leaned back in his chair, stretching. "A wise man knows when his luck has deserted him."

"Or when it rides with him?"

"True," admitted the mercenary. "Like that time on Tchang when the charge of my laser had bled and I only had an automatic gun and a score of cartridges between me and what I knew was extinction. When I ran into an enemy patrol, I tried to open fire and the damned thing jammed solid. I thought I was dead for sure, but what I didn't know was that peace had been signed shortly before and, had I hit anyone, I'd have been impaled for breaking the truce. That was good luck and I tried to ride it by buying that damned mine. I thought I finally had it made; just work a little, dig out some metal, hire some men to dig out more and I'd live easy the rest of my life. But I was cheated. Even so, I was still lucky. If I hadn't bought the mine I'd have been with my old company when they got themselves wiped out with flames in the Hitach-Lentil war on Loom." He sat, brooding, his seamed face sagging, suddenly old. "Flamers," he whispered. "A hell of a way to go."

Men screaming, their clothing a mass of flame, skin bursting into a mass of oozing blisters, blood smoking as it spouted from ruptured veins. Eyes gone. Feet destroyed. Lungs gone. Hands turned into shreds of brittle, yet still living, bone. Feet destroyed. Faces.

Unsteadily he rose and crossed the room toward the spigots, the water, the basic which provided a liquid diet, the weak wine which, too slowly, could bring a blessed oblivion.

The recording had ended; the thin, keening notes accompanied by the muffled beat of drums had died into silence and now only the smoke remained. Jumoke drew it deeply into his lungs, savoring its bite, the euphoria it would give, the forgetfulness. And yet, some things refused to die; the touch of a hand, a smile, the feel of warm, lovely flesh. A whispered word, a promise implied if not spoken, a yearning which was like a pain.

Was a pain. One which tore at his heart and stung his eyes with unshed tears; which closed about the innermost core of his being so that, in his mind, he cried out for the universe to hear.

Dilys—I love you! I love you!

And would always love her. Would always want her with a need which went beyond sane logic and calculated reason. His woman. His life.

The smoke curled about his face, fumes rising from the can before which he squatted, chemical heat releasing the vapors from exotic compounds, a mist which should have brought a roseate glow. One destroyed now by the pounding, the echo of drums, the voice which rose then exploded as Allain burst into the cabin.

"Jumoke! Are you crazy? The Old Man would kill you if he saw you like this."

The Old Man? Which old man? Who was talking and why? Questions which shattered like broken glass as the steward grabbed him, lifted him, thrust his head beneath a faucet and let a mist of water spray over head and neck as he snuffed the can. Glass which became reality to the sting of astringent odors as Allain thrust something beneath his nose, became pain as the man slapped his face, turned into anger at his cursing.

"That's enough!"

"Like hell it is! You know what you're doing? It's my neck too, remember. You dumb bastard, I've a mind to—"

"I said that's enough!" Jumoke straightened, water dewing his face, vanishing as he used the towel Allain handed to him. "What's the matter? Trouble?"

"You're due to go on duty."

"So soon?"

"You should have reported ten minutes ago. Varn sent me to get you." Allain glanced at the can with its gaudy label and insidious contents. "I'll tell him you overslept if he should ask, and you'd better tell him the same. But if you try a stupid thing like this again, I'll break both your arms. You'd better believe that."

"I want no favors from you."

"You're getting them, just the same." Stepping closer, Allain said quietly, "Get a grip on yourself, man. You can't act like this in the Rift and you know it. Still less, in the Quillian

Sector. If you want to commit suicide, then wait until after we've landed."

Jumoke said coldly, "You forget yourself. I'm the navigator and you're nothing but a damned steward."

"I'm a partner, and even if I wasn't I wouldn't let a friend make such a fool of himself. What is it, man? Can't you get her out of your mind?"

He knew, of course, as Gresham had known and Egulus must know. How could they have remained ignorant when his happiness had illuminated the ship? When his world had been complete and he had been free of the pain which rode him now. The loss. The yearning. The endless, empty yearning.

Damn her!

Damn her all to hell!

And damn Dumarest with her!

Egulus stared hard at him as Jumoke entered the control room. The captain looked tired, eyes betraying the strain he was under, the need to remain constantly alert, which was the price of survival for any officer traversing the Rift.

"You're late."

"I know, Varn. I'm sorry. I overslept."

Egulus accepted the lie, though his nostrils twitched as the navigator passed him to take his place in the main chair. A captain needed to know what went on in his vessel and Egulus was no fool, but there was a time to be hard and a time to compromise. And now, more than ever, he needed the navigator.

"We're running into a lot of distortion," he said. "Those suns are playing up and space is a mess. Nodes and vortexes all over the place. We'd best cut shifts so as to remain alert. I'll send Allain up with something to help."

Drugs to wash away the fatigue and the residue of the vapors. Chemicals to steal time from the need to sleep, a debt which would have to be paid for later but which would buy them a higher margin of safety. A common practice in dangerous areas of space.

"I'll be all right."

"Did I suggest otherwise?"

"You don't have to worry about me, Varn." Jumoke turned to meet the captain's eyes. "Go and get some rest now."

"Yes," said Egulus. "Yes, I guess you're right. Rest is what I need."

Rest and more crew, so as to lessen the burden, and the sense to quit the game while he was still ahead. While he still had his life. A familiar thought, and one he treasured like an old friend, but one he would never listen to when the danger was past. As the others, whose bodies drifted in the Rift, hadn't listened. Captains who had gambled once too often. Ships which had crumpled like paper bags when caught in the invisible jaws of the monster which lurked always just beyond the hull.

Alone, Jumoke checked the instruments, eyes moving with the ease of long practice from dial to meter, from digital readout to the shades of color seething behind graduated scales. Sensors which, even now, were questing space around and ahead. Probes which checked the local stresses and warned of opposed potentials. Electronic eyes which guided the hurtling vessel through the vagaries of the plus-C universe through which it moved, powered and protected by the shimmering haze of its Erhaft field.

A touch and a meter swung to optimum, a minor adjustment and a dial settled from its nervous twitching. Things done even as Jumoke breathed, actions taken without the hampering need for conscious thought. A game he played to beat the computer which would have made the necessary correction had the variation grown dangerously wild.

The control room was dimly lit, the glow of telltales like colorful, watching eyes, the soft susurration of the air-circulators, the breathing of a thing alive. It was easy to imagine the room as being a womb, the ship as a living thing. A temptation to give it anthropomorphic attributes. A woman with the computer for a brain and the engines for a heart. The sensors, stalked and staring eyes. The probes, reaching hands. The crew, the seed carried in her belly.

Would he give her a child?

The thought was like the thrust of a knife into his guts, a blade which turned and dragged and spilled his life so that he doubled and felt the vomit rise in his throat.

Not that! Dear God, not that!

Because that would be the end and the death of all hope that she would come back to him, to rest at his side as she had done so often before, to let his hands rove over her soft and tender body, touching, fondling, caressing, lingering on the swell of breasts and the curve of thighs, the softness between them, the moist wonder which had once been his.

Madness. The whine of a child. He knew it, and knowing it, could do nothing about it, for what else was a man obsessed but a crying child? One who wanted more than could be given—and yet he asked so little. The opportunity to love, to worship, to share.

A hope which had died even as he voiced it.

Leaning back, he saw her face painted against the screens, the incredible splendor of the universe they portrayed; the stars and clouds, the sheets of luminescence and curtains of radiance. The fuzz of distant nebulae, the splinters and pulses and flares. Loveliness to match her own. A coldness she shared.

"No, Jumoke." He had cringed to the iron resolve of her tone. "No."

"But, Dilys, where's the harm? We've known each other for so long and you know I love you. Why let a stranger ruin what we have between us?"

"Had," she corrected. "We've nothing now, Jumoke."

"I—we, for God's sake, Dilys! Must I beg? All right, I'm begging. I need you. Please!"

"No." Then, looking at him, she had softened a little. "We shared something, yes, but that was all. It was a physical thing, a convenience, if you like. We both needed release and each could give it to the other. But now you ask too much."

"Dilys—"

"I'm not a whore!"

"Did I say you were? But on Aclyte and Nyard women take multiple husbands. They are shared by the men. Do I ask for so much?"

"You ask too much."

"But—" He had sought for words with which to win her. A phrase to buy happiness. "Dumarest is just a man, as I am. What makes him so different?"

"I love him." She had reached out then, and touched his cheek, her fingers burning even as they felt like ice. "I love him, Jumoke. I love him!"

The face vanished and he sank into hell.

He would never win her back. Never again feel the pride he had known. Never again the happiness. She had taken

them from him and given them to another. Dumarest.
Jumoke lifted his hands and looked at them, clenched, the
skin taut over the knuckles. Dumarest, Dumarest and Dilys—
he wished both were dead.

"Now!" Gale Andrel turned a switch and the salon
bloomed with light. "The Garden of Emdale," she said. "It is
one of my favorites."

Which was why she carried the recording with her—much
of what she did and said was obvious, a trait Bochner had
noted and assessed as a part of her facade. One of apparent
childish exuberance, probably adopted to match her innocent
face. But there was nothing innocent about her as he now
knew. Within the slight figure burned a mature passion but
both it and her body had left him curiously unsatisfied. A trophy won, a symbolical kill made, yet there had been small
joy in the victory. Like swatting a fly, it had been too easy.
An act performed from boredom, and as an aid to his as-
sumed character. A prop he wished he had done without.

But, in other ways, the woman had skill.

"It's beautiful!" The dancer was entranced. She spun, arms
extended, the transformation of the salon giving her an elfin
grace. "Beautiful!"

Even Charl Zeda had to agree, his voice gruff as he added
to her praise. "It's fantastic! My dear, allow me to congratu-
late you. To honor you in the accustomed manner."

She turned her lips from his kiss, allowing him only to
touch her cheek and, watching, Bochner could sense her tension, the repugnance she felt towards the old mercenary.
Would she have reacted the same if Dumarest had offered his
salutation?

Bochner glanced to where he stood behind the table, his
back to the wall. The sight pleased him; the stance was that
of a cautious man. Only when he had marked his prey did
the hunter allow himself to study the hologram which had
been created by the projector and the woman's art.

Gale had chosen well. On all sides stood a profusion of
flowers touched with a multitude of hues, reds and greens
and blues merging with violets and scarlets and purples and
all degrees of the shades between. Alone, that would have
been impressive, but the blooms were in motion, kissed by an
unfelt breeze, their cups the targets for wide-winged insects

which flashed and shimmered, to hang poised to flash again in metallic gleams which entranced the eye as their drone excited the ear.

And, almost, he could smell the flowers.

They filled his vision, numbing his eyes with their form and brilliance, a poem in color augmented by the insects so that it was hard not just to sit and stare and let the tide of beauty roll over him and become one with the moment. He became aware that the salon was silent aside from the thin hum of the insects. Almost, it could have been filled with the dead. Then he saw the historian, the man's eyes enormous in his pallid face, a creature stunned and enamored by loveliness beyond all his previous experience.

Quietly, Bochner moved from the salon, heading down the passage, past the cabin he occupied, past the one shared by the mercenary and historian, the one in which Andrel slept when she chose to rest alone, the one hired by the dancer, that which formed the steward's office to halt at the door which gave onto Dumarest's quarters. It swung open as he manipulated the lock, and he stepped inside to stand as his eyes searched the compartment.

Here? Would it be here? The thing Dumarest owned which made him so valuable to the Cyclan that they had hired him to hunt him down.

He saw nothing but the usual furnishings; the bed, the cabinet, the washbowl with its spray faucet. A chair stood against the bulkhead and a small boxlike container rested to the side of the bed, close to the head. It held a door, which he opened. Behind lay gray plastic clothing, neatly folded, high boots of matching color, a knife.

Bochner lifted it and straightened as he examined the weapon.

It was a tool designed for service, the blade nine-inches long, curved, the reverse side sweeping in a sharper curve so as to form a vicious, needle-point. The guard was smooth on the inside, rough on the outside with a pattern of engraved lines, a means of catching an opposed blade. The hilt was shaped, wrapped with plastic, topped with a rounded pommel. Bochner examined it, twisting it, finding it firm and noting the thin line of weld lying in the junction of pommel and hilt. He balanced it in his palm, feeling the distribution of weight, the heft. A good blade, he decided. One deadly in an

experienced hand. Along the edge, the light splintered to
form a cloudlike haze—the sign of sharpness, of keenness so
well-achieved that it equaled that of a surgeon's scalpel.

"You! What are you doing here?" The woman was sharp.
Bochner turned as she entered the cabin, the knife poised in
his hand. "That isn't yours," Dilys accused. "What are you
doing with it?"

"I was curious."

"Curious enough to break into another's cabin?"

"The door was open," he lied. "I glanced in as I passed
and saw this knife. I am a hunter and have an interest in
weapons. An interest which overcame my discretion, I'm
afraid. I couldn't resist examining it. Earl's?"

"Yes."

"As I thought. Dumarest is the kind of man who would
know how to use it. The kind of man I have a need of." He
saw the flicker of interest in her eyes and, replacing the knife,
he closed the door of the boxlike cabinet. Now, if he could
get them both out of the cabin, the door relocked and Dilys
so intrigued that she would fail to mention the incident to her
lover, he would have won. "After you, my dear."

Impelled by his hand, she stepped outside and watched as
he closed the door. He was fortunate, the panel had a spring
lock. The game won, then, but the victory was nothing. It
would be better if she warned Dumarest—a quarry on its
guard made for better sport. And yet, only a fool made a
stalk more difficult than it needed to be.

She said, "What did you mean when you said you needed
a man like Earl?"

The bait had been nibbled, gently he tightened the line.

"In my work. As you probably know, I am associated with
a consortium of speculators interested in expanding into
wider fields. We cater to those who like to hunt, and are always in need of men who have both knowledge and experience in the field. Someone to arrange for various safaris. To
guide and guard our customers, not all of whom are as
knowledgeable as we would like." His smile and gesture made
clear his meaning. "Dumarest would be ideal. He is a man
who inspires confidence and seems to have an innate caution
and an awareness of what needs to be done when it needs to
be done. A perfect hunter, guide, guardian and teacher. On
Persing, he—but what is the use?"

"Persing?"

"Yes. A world we are opening up for exploitation. It has magnificent hills ideal for breeding predators and good cover for those who have a wish to hunt them. A stalk, properly managed, could take days. We need a manager, someone to oversee the workers, to maintain the beasts, to decide on the hunts. In short, someone to take full charge. There is a house of thirty rooms, the use of a raft, servants and the renumeration is generous. That isn't taking into account the usual gifts made by satisfied clients. And there is always the prospect of promotion."

"Which are . . ."

"Very good. As I told you, we are expanding and there is room for a good man to climb high and reach the top. Frankly, I'd like Earl to be that man, but I guess to hope for that is to hope for too much. Well, that's the way it goes." Then, casually, he added, "Of course, he would need to be married before we could consider him for the position."

"Married?"

"It makes for stability. A man with a wife and children is more likely to stay than one who hasn't. You can see our point of view? To furnish a large house, to make all the arrangements and then, because of some passing fancy, to be let down—" His shrug was eloquent. "You are close?"

He would have been a fool not to have known it but she could appreciate his delicacy.

"We are friends, yes."

"He is a lucky man. Shall we join the others?"

Bochner took her arm, aware of her presence as he had never felt the presence of another of her sex. Not simply because of her femininity, which was strong, or her size, which was unusual, but because of something to do with his own conditioning. The natural reaction of a man who had felt superior, both in height and ability, to all others for the majority of his life. It did not please him to feel dwarfed.

Yet, he maintained his smile. The woman was just another game, another hunt. To bend her to his will, to manipulate, to delude, to misguide, to dangle the lure of golden promises—all were part of the sport.

As they walked down the passage, he said, "One thing, my dear, a matter of confidence. I would not like Earl to know how eager I am to obtain his services. A business precaution,

you understand. It would be best if he knew nothing of what
I told you." Than, casually, he added, "Has he ever spoken
of leaving the *Entil*?"

"No."

"But he surely doesn't intend to remain for long?"

"I—I don't know."

He caught the note of doubt, the inner worry which she
must strive to conceal, and felt increased amusement. How
simple some people were. How transparent was a woman in
love.

"It must be in his mind," said Bochner. "A world he would
like to make his home. One he may have mentioned to you.
Aaras, perhaps, or Vien." Both were on the edge of the Sector, though still within the Rift. Logical places for a man like
Dumarest to make a change. "Swenna, perhaps?"

"No," she said, a little too quickly. "The only world he's
mentioned is Earth."

"Earth?"

"He was joking, of course."

"Of course." Bochner yielded precedence as they reached
the door leading to the salon. "After you, my dear."

Allain came toward her as she stepped inside. He looked
like a ghost in a living garden; walking through the tumult of
flowers, the glint of metallic wings adding extra eyes to the
tension of his face. He caught her arm and drew her from
the salon.

"Jumoke—have you seen him?"

"No." She sensed his urgency. "Is something wrong?"

"Varn wants him. The instruments are acting all to hell,
and he's worried. Jumoke could be responsible. He—"

"Jumoke commit sabotage? That's impossible!"

"Once, yes, but now I'm not so sure." The steward was bitter. "He's been eating smoke and God alone knows what
other things. The man's half-crazed and not even seeing
straight. I've tried to cover for him, but now he's gone too
far. Have you seen him? I've checked the salon but he isn't
there. His cabin?"

"Maybe." She made her decision. "I'll look—he'll answer
for me."

Answer, if he was inside and read more into her call than
was intended, but that was a problem to be settled later.
Now, with the ship in potential risk, there was no time for

worry about personal commitments. As a crew, all had to stick and operate together.

But he wasn't inside. The door remained closed and, when she opened it with the master key, the cabin was empty aside from the acrid taint of drugged vapors.

"Smoke," said Allain, grimly. "He must have hidden some away. I thought I'd found every can."

"The instruments," she said. "Just what is the situation?"

"Bad. Varn's doing his best, but Jumoke is the navigator. We're off-course as it is, and surrounded by trouble. At the best, days have been added to the journey. The worst—" He didn't need to complete the sentence. "Where the hell is he?"

A jerk gave the answer. A slight movement of the deck beneath their feet, a twitch of the hull, a movement of the fabric itself, as if the ship had shrugged within its skin.

Varn Egulus felt it and reared in his chair, his face ghastly in the subdued light of the telltales. The historian felt it and shrugged, happy in his ignorance. Gale Andrel pursed her lips as the hologram shook a little, then steadied to its former beauty. Bochner felt it and guessed. Dumarest felt it and knew.

As did the dancer who halted the undulating movements of her arms, the complex pattern she wove among the blaze of flowers to stand, mouth open, the scarlet smear of a bloom casting the semblance of blood over her throat and chest, a blotch which quivered as she screamed.

"The ship! My God, the ship! The field is down!"

Chapter Seven

———————

Jumoke lay where he had died, looking very small now, a limp figure with burned and blackened hands and a face which had one cheek pressed hard against the bulk of the generator which he had ruined. A face still tormented by the devils which had possessed him, one unrelaxed by the peace he had hoped to gain.

"The bastard!" Allain was bitter. "If he wanted to die, why take us with him?"

"He was crazy," said Dilys. "You said so yourself."

"And who sent him that way?" The steward's anger was the product of fear. "You could have given in to him. Let him have you and kept him sane."

"I'm not property. The ship doesn't own me."

"Where would have been the harm? You went with him before and you knew how he felt. You could have lied, promised, given him hope. Damn it, a kiss could have saved us!"

"That's enough," said Dumarest. "Dilys isn't at fault. If anyone is to blame, it's you. You knew he was eating smoke. Why didn't you stop him?"

"I tried."

"Like hell you tried!" Dilys flared with a sudden rage. "Did you report it to Varn? Did you tell anyone? Did you take precautions against something like this happening?" She gestured to the body, the machine. "Damn you, Allain. Damn you!"

Dumarest caught her lifted hand before she could send its palm against the steward's cheek. For a moment, she struggled with him and he felt the strength of her, the fear and anger which powered the muscles beneath the skin, then,

90

abruptly, she was against him, her face pressed against his own, a dampness on her cheek.

"Earl! Oh, Earl!"

He held her, waiting for the moment to pass, knowing that until it did, nothing constructive could be done. When she finally straightened, he said, "How bad is the damage? Can it be fixed?"

"I don't know. I'll have to check."

"Then get on with it." Stopping, Dumarest gripped the body and swung it to one side. "Allain, you'd better get back to the passengers. Give them tranquilizers if they need them, and any lies which can give them comfort. We've had a temporary breakdown which will take a little while to fix. In the meantime, they can enjoy the hospitality of the ship. Break out some spirits and strong wines. Euphoriants, too, and get that woman to play more of her recordings."

"They aren't stupid, Earl. They know what it means once the field is down."

As they all knew—knowledge which gave no peace of mind. Once the shimmering haze of the Erhaft field was down the ship dropped to below light speed, to drift in the immensity between the stars, to be vulnerable to any wandering scrap of debris which might cross their path—motes which could penetrate the hull and larger fragments which would vent their kinetic energy in a fury which would turn metal into vapor. And there were other dangers, less tangible, but more to be feared. The impact of invisible energies which could twist and distort the vessel and all within it, forces which were thick in the area they now traversed.

"Dilys?"

"I'm working as fast as I can, Earl." She was at the generator, tools spread in orderly confusion around her, hands grimed, as was her face, her hair. She had stripped off her blouse and wore nothing above the waist but the fabric confining her breasts. They, and the flesh of back and shoulders, glistened with perspiration. "He'd loosed the covers," she said. "Lifted them and put something inside. A scrap of wire which he used to short out the coils."

"So?"

"Like Allain said, the poor devil was crazed. He must have wanted to attract my attention in some way."

"He wanted to die."

"Perhaps not, Earl. He didn't know too much about generators. He needn't have meant to do much damage."

"He wanted to die and take us with him." To Dumarest it was obvious and he wondered why she would want to think of excuses for her ex-lover. Because of that, perhaps, a reluctance to think ill of someone who had been so close. "Is there anything I can do to help?"

For answer, she shook her head. He had done enough, dragging the dead body into the hold and cycling it through the lock. Dead meat, fit only to be dumped into the void, but once it had been a man and one she could have saved had she been less harsh. Allain had been right. A kiss could have saved them all.

A kiss, and a little less carelessness on her part.

Had she not left the engine room untended. Hadn't wandered down the passage to enter Dumarest's cabin and waste time talking to Bochner. Hadn't become enamored of the picture he had painted, the house and prospects, the position he'd mentioned. The one dependent on marriage. Would Earl have married her to make himself eligible?

Was he a man who could be bought?

Questions which now had no meaning. Looking into the interior of the generator, she could see the damage which Jumoke had caused; delicate installations now seared and blacked, insulation charred, surfaces which should have gleamed like mirrors now dulled with the impact of heat, stained by condensed vapors. Things which could be repaired, and would be repaired if given the time, but the main problem was within the triple helixes. Each set at right angles to the other, things of delicate fabrication, matched to within five decimal places of similarity. How badly had they been distorted?

It would take instruments to tell. Tests and calibrations, and more tests with the instruments she had at hand and the knowledge she had acquired. But, to retune them was another matter. To match them so they would restore the field, was a matter of luck and skill and time. Luck, in that they weren't too badly damaged. Skill, to sense and adjust and manipulate and balance. Time, in which to work.

Time!

Egulus shook his head when Dumarest made his report.

"We haven't the time, Earl. That bastard did a good job on

us. He worked on the instruments before heading for the generator. I guess he wanted to get us in any way he could."

The captain was being generous—Jumoke had only been interested in killing the engineer and her new lover.

"Radio?"

"Out. I don't mean we just can't get messages in the Quillian Sector. That's bad enough, but at least we might have been lucky. No. The crazy idiot took care of that. Busted it all to hell and the spare unit with it. I guess we should be thankful he didn't wreck the screens while he was at it."

A small advantage, and of dubious merit. Had the screens been wrecked they would have been "blind" but as it was, they could see the cold hostility of the universe in which they now drifted helplessly. See the flare of a nearby sun and the ugly corona around it, the leaping prominences, the blotches of roiling vapors which gave it a pocked appearance as if it were a thing alive and horribly diseased.

"We're heading towards it," said Egulus, "and without power we're going to hit it. Jumoke's last gift to his friends and partners." His hands closed as if he could feel a throat. "I was too gentle," he said bitterly. "I smelled the stink of that smoke but never thought he would be such a fool. To lose his head over a woman!"

"That's all you noticed? The smoke?"

"He was tense and withdrawn, but that's normal when in the Rift. To make a living, we have to take chances and always something can go wrong. It's worse in the Quillian Sector, but you know about that. We make profits but we earn them." He ended bleakly. "Greed. It's killed more men than anything else. The temptation to make an easy profit. To take that one extra chance."

"Kumetat?"

"We didn't have to go there. I was going to give it a miss this time and hit it on the way back in. Only there was a cargo, and how could I refuse?"

An odd cargo for a desert world, Dumarest remembered, but odd things were carried at times. And he'd had no choice but to stay with the *Entil*. The worlds at which it had touched had been too backward for plentiful shipping. Too undeveloped for a man to earn the price of another passage. Bad worlds on which to be stranded. Hard planets to easily leave. Impossible places on which to hide.

"And if we hadn't got that cargo?"

"We'd be on Tullon by now. At least, that's where we were headed until we touched at Kumetat. They had an urgent delivery for Mucianus. A good world. One on the rim of the Sector and close to the edge of the Rift. We could have stayed awhile, a day or two, maybe. There's always a choice of cargoes." He ended bitterly, "Now it looks as if we're going to roast in hell."

The Garden of Emdale had gone, the bright colors vanished, the flowers, the darting insects, all had disappeared. They had been followed by the chill mistiness of the Chephron Gorge, with its souring walls and looming masses, its blurred details and rocks stained and weathered with time and climate so as to give the appearance of ranked and leering skulls. Other recordings had followed, and now she sat engulfed by the glittering magic of the Elg Cavern. A place of winking points of variegated hue as crystals caught and reflected a mote of light, amplifying it, splintering it into a hundred component parts, distorting it, filling the salon with a snowstorm of sparkles, of eye-catching joy.

But now they gave her no pleasure. Nothing now could give her pleasure. She was filled with the knowledge that she was to die.

What had she said to Bochner?

An end. An extinction. The total erasure of a personal universe. The termination of existence.

And he had called it a form of beauty!

She looked to where she had seen him last, but failed to spot him in the flickering showers of brilliance. At the table, perhaps? Talking to Threnond about his wares? A stupidity, if he was—how could there be interest now in instruments of death? Better to buy some of Fele Roster's compounds. They, at least, could bring sweet dreams and illusions and a release from the fear of death.

And she was afraid.

God, she was afraid!

"Here!" The mercenary loomed beside her, his scarred face grotesque in the splintering glitters. He lifted the bottle in his hand and she could smell the alcohol on his breath. "Have a drink," he urged. "The steward's been generous. The best, and all free."

"No."

"Drugs then? He—"

"No," she said again, and then added, "Please, I'd rather sit alone."

"In the salon?" His tone was dry and she realized that he was far less drunk then he seemed. "Haven't you a cabin?"

"Charl, you're an opportunist." The dancer had joined them, her eyes glittering, mouth twisted in a smile. "But she's too young for you."

"I was offering her a drink."

"And asking for payment, eh?" She gave a harlot's laugh. "Reminding her that time is short and not to be wasted. Asking about her cabin. Hinting that one more experience can do her no harm and do you a lot of good. Why her? Can't I give as much as she can?"

He said flatly, "You've a dirty mouth."

"To match your dirty hands! Mercenaries! Scum! Killers of women and children! Murderers!" The slap of an open hand preceded her scream of anger. "Bastard! You hit me! I'll—"

A scuffle, a muffled sound, and the mercenary swore before he collapsed, his eyes vague, the bottle falling to spill its contents on the floor. The dancer picked it up, laughing, lost in her drugged euphoria. She had used the wrong ring, the man would recover and be none the worse for his experience, but if he struck her again she would make no mistake. A dart in his throat or one in his eye. One for the uppity young bitch who played with light. And the third?

The third she would save for herself.

Allain said, "They're getting restless, Earl. I've given them drink and drugs but they know there's little hope. People act oddly when they know they're going to die. Some try to cram everything into the last few days. Some just sit and look at their hands. Some pray. Some even commit suicide. Can you understand that? They kill themselves because they are certain they are going to die."

"Everyone has to die."

"That's what I mean. Why anticipate it?" The steward shrugged with strained bravado. His face was a little too tense, his eyes a little too bright, but he had a responsibility and recognized it. And some of the hope he disseminated among the passengers had stuck. Death was something which happened to others. Always it happened to others. "The generator?"

"Nothing, as yet."

"Maybe if I helped?"

"You can't help." Dumarest, understanding, was patient. "It's all up to Dilys."

She'd worked like a machine, drugs giving her a temporary reprieve from the need to sleep, other compounds robbing tissue and nerve to provide a chemical strength. Now, she took the steaming cup Dumarest handed to her and gulped at the protein-rich fluid, sickly sweet with glucose and laced with vitamins. A second cup of basic followed the first. She waved aside a third.

"No more, Earl. You'll have me as fat as a pig."

"You need the energy. It's been a long time."

"Yes." She set down the container and glanced at the bulk of the generator. Dark rings of fatigue circled her eyes and her hands held a slight tremble. She looked at them, splaying the fingers, examining her cracked nails, the tips stained with acid, torn with abrasives. "How long, Earl? Five days?"

"Seven." A week, during which time she hadn't slept and had rarely eaten. The food he had given her was the prelude to the exhausted sleep which would follow. "Here." Dumarest handed her a glass filled with a smoky amber fluid. "Brandy, and Allain tells me it's the best. From his own private stock." He added, "He has reserved another bottle—one with poison."

The final drink, but one which she knew he wouldn't share. Death, when it came, would be met by Dumarest with open eyes. He would fight it as he had fought it all his life. Facing impossible odds because, no matter how high they were against him, there was always the chance that, somehow, he could win.

Lifting the glass, she said, "You'll join me?"

"In a toast, yes." Dumarest raised a second glass. "To success!"

"I can't guarantee that. Let us drink to hope."

"To success," he insisted. "Nothing else will do."

A fact she knew too well, and she drank, slowly, feeling the warmth of the spirit sting her mouth and throat and trace a warm path to her stomach. Conscious, too, of the fatigue which dulled her mind and made every muscle an aching irri-

tation. Had she done all that needed to be done? The cleaning? The coils? The connections? The adjustments? Had a
tool been overlooked? A scrap of wire? A shred of metal, or
a fragment of insulation? Work had slowed as the hours had
passed and it was easy to overlook the obvious when tired.

"Dilys?" She jerked, aware that she had been dozing, on
the edge of sleep. Dumarest said, "If you've finished your
drink, let's find out how good an engineer you are."

The drink—the remains rested in her glass and she emptied
it with a single swallow. A silent toast to the oblivion which
could be waiting at the turn of a switch. A silent prayer to
the gods of chance on whose laps they now all rested.
Dumarest was right, they could use nothing less than success.

Had she achieved it?

There was only one way to find out.

She took a step forward and swayed, and felt the edge of
the workbench press hard against her spine as she moved
back against it. She sagged, welcoming the support, shaking
her head as Dumarest came toward her.

"No, Earl, I can't. I'm beat. You do it. Everything's set—
just throw the switches."

She watched as he obeyed, hearing the generator hum into
life, feeling a success which blazed through her so powerfully
that she straightened and smiled her triumph; a smile which
died as the hum faltered, to steady, to falter again.

"I've failed," she smiled dully. "I tried but I wasn't good
enough. The damned generator isn't going to last."

The place held the memory of summer flowers, of fields
graced with blossoms harvested by smiling girls, to be taken
and treated and condensed into vials of concentrated joy.
Traces of perfume which held the stamp of the one who had
worn it. Dilys, lying now on her bed, her face flaccid, the
curves of her figure like those of an erotic dream.

Dumarest tightened the restraints, which held her in broad
bands of yielding webbing to her cot. Extra thicknesses of
mattresses lay beneath her and he had arranged further padding so as to coccoon her within the restraints. Her condition
made his task easy; drugged, deep in exhausted unconsciousness, she had barely stirred as he'd worked.

A woman who had burned herself out. Who had done her

best and discovered it wasn't good enough. An added ingredient to Jumoke's revenge.

Outside the cabin Dumarest paused, looking along the passage. Allain emerged from a door, curses following him fading as he closed the panel. The dancer spitting her venom.

"She's drunk," the steward explained, "but not drunk enough. God, what a hag!"

"You've put her in restraints?"

"I tried, but she fought like a wildcat. Well, to hell with her."

"Try again later," said Dumarest. "If she's drunk, she isn't responsible. The rest?"

"Warned and as ready as they'll ever be. Now I'm going to look after myself." The steward hesitated. "Do you think we'll make it?"

"If the generator holds out, yes."

"And if it doesn't?" Allain answered his own question. "We burn, we drift, we starve. If we're lucky, we die quick."

"Or we live," said Dumarest. "Luck comes in two kinds."

"Sure, that's what I mean. With good luck we go out easy—with bad we linger. Well, to hell with it. I'm going to hit the bottle."

He headed for his own cabin as Dumarest moved on. As he entered the control room, Egulus said, "Dilys?"

"Still out. I wrapped her well."

"The others?" The captain shrugged as he heard the report. "Passengers! At times they act as if they're crazy. Well, they've had their warning. My main concern now is with the *Entil*."

A crippled ship, now heading towards an isolated world. Taking his place in the navigator's chair, Dumarest could see it in the screens, a mottled ball of green and ocher, patched with expanses of dingy white, streaked with smears of dusty black.

"That's Hyrcanus, as far as I can make out," said Egulus. "But right or wrong, it's the only chance we have. We make it or burn." He glanced at the sun, which blazed with awesome splendor. "But if the generator holds, we've a chance."

One which grew as the ball of the planet swelled larger, colors breaking into a blurred jumble, the instruments in the control room clicking as they relayed information.

Closer, and the ship began to shudder a little as opposed gravities fought for supremacy. A slight shift told of a dying vortex, spewed from some flaring sun. A peculiar turning sensation as it passed through an area of intra-dimensional instability. The normal hazards to be expected within the Rift.

Another which was not.

Egulus swore as the ship died beneath his hands. "The generator! It's dead!"

Strained beyond endurance by the impact of external forces, the interior now a mass of fused and molten rubbish, the Erhaft field gone, and this time never to be replaced.

And the world was close.

Close!

Dumarest said, "The directional vents, are they working?"

"Yes, thank God."

"Then skip! Skip!"

The only chance they had and one which the captain had already assessed. Now, as they fell towards the mass of the planet below, Egulus proved his skill. In order to kill their velocity and to prevent being burned by the atmosphere, he had to maintain height while remaining within orbit. To use the air-blanket as a boy would a pond. To send the ship skimming over it as if it were a flung stone, touching, bouncing, touching again.

The hull turned red as air blasted over it with a thin, high scream, a scream echoed from somewhere within the vessel. Both screams died as Egulus operated the vents, lifting the ship a fraction, letting it hurtle on to drop again, to glow as it had before, to lift and pray and curse as dials showed red and alarm bells shrilled their warning.

"Kill that damned noise!"

Sweat dripped from Dumarest's face as he hit the switches. The hull screamed again as the bells fell silent, the shriek maintained as the air grew hotter, became stifled, became a searing torment.

"Up! Up, damn you!"

"I can't! I—" Egulus hit the controls, feeding extra power into the vents, praying ever as he worked, prayers which sounded like curses as, slowly, the screaming died and, velocity killed, the *Entil* fell towards the surface below.

Dumarest watched as the ground streamed past on the screens. They needed a flat and even expanse, covered with soft dirt, sand, snow, stunted vegetation, even ice. A place on which to skid for miles until they came to a halt and, even then, such a landing would be close to a miracle.

"Nothing." Egulus snarled his anger. "The damned place is a nightmare!"

Hills, crevasses, chasms, stony wilderness with boulders like waiting teeth, trees resting on the edges of precipices, plains marked with undulating serrations like the teeth of saws.

"Water," said Dumarest. "We need water."

It showed ahead and a little to one side, a long narrow inlet which opened to the grayness of a sea. A strand, and it was below and before them, choppy waves bearing patches of kelp and whiteness caused by spume thrown from upthrust rocks. Then they were over it.

"Down," yelled Dumarest. "Down, man, down!"

They were going too fast, but ahead he had caught the loom of mountains standing etched against the sky. Pillars of stone too high for them to surmount and too widespread to avoid. The choice between hitting them and plunging into the sea was no choice at all.

No choice, but a gamble, and one Egulus took as he had when entering the atmosphere. The *Entil* tilted a little, headed downwards, hit the water to bounce as it had when meeting the atmosphere. Steam rose, created by the impact of hot metal, the vapor forming a cushion between the water and the hull.

Bouncing, skipping, as the mountains came closer. As the vessel creaked and shuddered and blood ran from ears and noses, as soft flesh suffered from the savage buffeting.

To hit for the last time. To sink. To hit bottom, to lift a little, to settle again and come to a final rest.

After an eternity, Varn Egulus said, "No water. The hull remained intact." He sounded as if he couldn't believe it.

"Luck," said Dumarest.

"For us, maybe." The captain wiped the back of his hand over his face and looked at the blood. "For the others?"

Chapter Eight

The historian was dead—torn from his restraints to be flung against the hull, to roast, to die screaming in his pain. The dancer was dead, lying wrapped in her cocoon, hands lifted, the ugly blotches of disintegration marring throat and torso. Craters made by the darts from the ring she had carelessly continued to wear, fired by the involuntary contractions of her finger. An irony she seemed to appreciate as she stared upwards with blind eyes, her mouth twisted in the rictus of a smile. The steward was dead, lying in a crumpled heap, a bottle miraculously unbroken in his hand. The special bottle, which was to have been saved to the very last. One he had taken by mistake, perhaps, but his lips bore no smile. Unlike the dancer, he failed to appreciate the jest.

The rest were alive, bruised but otherwise unhurt aside from Charl Zeda. He sucked in his breath, sweat breaking out in globules on his seamed face, as Dumarest used leverage to ease the mercenary's badly dislocated shoulder back into position.

"That's better." Gently he tested the joint. "I was a fool, moved at the wrong time and got caught by one of the decelerations. How's the ship?" He frowned at the answer. "Under the surface, no generator, no power to lift—how the hell are we to get out?"

A question repeated by Gale Andrel when, later, they had gathered in the salon.

"We can get out," said Dumarest. "All we need to do is to cycle through the air-lock in the cargo hold. But there are other considerations."

"Such as?"

"What to do once we are on the surface," said Leo Bochner quickly. He sat at the girl's side, his hand touching her own. "We could be a long way from shore and, without navigation aids, may not be able to tell in which direction it lies. Can you swim?"

"A little. Why?"

"A little, you say. How far is that? A mile? Ten? A score? Fifty?" Bochner shook his head. "A little isn't enough. We could be more than a hundred miles from land. Captain?"

"I don't know," admitted Egulus. "We came down fast and had other things to think about. Earl saw mountains ahead, but we were high at the time and they would be below the horizon now. In any case, they were far from close."

"And we must have traveled after we hit the ocean." Fele Roster pursed his lips, his eyes thoughtful. "How deep are we?"

"We hit bottom." Egulus shrugged at the other's expression. "I'm not sure how deep, the external gauge was burned, but from the time we took to descend, I'd say about four or five hundred feet."

"Deep," said Bochner. "Too deep for us to rise to the surface without difficulty."

"It would be impossible without protection," said Gale Andrel. "If we tried it we'd litter the surface with our bodies."

"Or provide food for the fish." Shan Threnond looked at his hands, the rings he had replaced gleaming in the light. "The fish and other things. Are you sure this world is Hyrcanus, Captain?"

"As near as I can figure, yes. You know it?"

"I've heard rumors." The dealer in death sucked at his lips, splinters of light darting from his rings to be reflected in little gleams from his eyes. "If they are to be believed, a wise man would do well to avoid this place."

"I've heard about it, too," rumbled Charl Zeda. He moved carefully in his chair, easing his sore shoulder. "A strange and savage world filled with unexpected perils. The mountains hold a peculiar form of life, and the seas are not as peaceful as they could be. The air, too—but every tavern is full of such whispers. If a man believed them all, he would never find the courage to travel."

"But if we are on Hyrcanus," said Threnond, "we had better think twice before trusting ourselves to the water. Even with what protection we can arrange, we'd stand small chance against what it could contain."

"If the rumors are true." Bochner shook his head. "Tales to frighten children. Stories spun by men while sitting half-drunk, in firelight. Yarns to interest women and to earn the price of another bottle. Stories about mythical worlds and beasts and treasures waiting to be found. You must have heard them, Earl?"

"Yes," said Dumarest. "Often."

"And never been tempted to investigate? To try and find Jackpot, say, with its fields of precious gems. Or Avalon with its scented breezes and singing flowers, with its food trees and wine streams and youth-restoring berries. Or Bonanza, with its veins of rich ores running like rainbows through the mountains. Never even tried to find Earth?"

Earth—the only world he had mentioned which he hadn't given a tinsel shine. And had his voice changed a little as he spoke the name? A coincidence? Perhaps, but Dumarest mistrusted coincidences.

"Earth," he said. "You know it?"

"Only as a legend, my friend. A name. One among a dozen. Shall I tell you of others? Of—"

"For God's sake!" Gale Andrel snapped her irritation. "To talk such rubbish at a time like this! What are we going to do? Are we to just sit here and wait? Will rescue come? Can it? Can we leave the ship? Can we reach land if we do?"

"Steady," said Bochner. "Steady."

"You—"

Her hand lifted, swung at his face, halted as he blocked it, the sound of slapped flesh sounding loud as his own fingers left red welts on her cheek. As she recoiled, eyes wide with shocked disbelief, he said, "I suggest you control yourself, my dear. And never attempt to strike me again."

"Was that necessary?" Dilys Edhessa glared her anger. "You spoke of terrors to be found on this world—must we add to them? Or do you consider it the height of courage to strike a defenseless woman?"

"A reaction. I—"

"Forgot yourself? Would you like to strike me?" She came toward him, overwhelming, eyes cold with her rage. "Try it," she invited. "Just try it—and I'll break your arm."

"You think you could do that?" He rose to face her, body

tense, poised, hands lifted as if to strike or parry as the need arose. The stance of a man accustomed to facing danger. That of the hunter he professed to be—or that of the fighter he had taken pains to hide.

Dumarest said, "Haven't we enough trouble as it is? Sit down, man. Dilys, what have you to report?"

For a moment she hesitated, then, as Bochner sat, she said, "The generator's out, as you know, and can't be repaired. We have power enough to run the life-support systems until we starve. We can recycle air and get water enough, but food is limited. Why, Earl? You knew all this."

"The other's didn't, or may have forgotten."

"So?" The last of her anger vanished with her shrug. "All right, I'm sorry. I should have managed to control myself. But I can't stand a man who hits women."

"Or a woman who kills men?" Dumarest met her eyes. "She could have a poisoned needle attached to her finger," he explained. "Or a lethal paste set beneath a sharpened nail. Like Bochner, I, too would have taken precautions had she slapped at my face."

"And slapped her back?"

"It's one way to teach a lesson." He changed the subject. "Have you anything which could be adapted to give underwater protection? Masks, air tanks, suits?"

"Tanks, yes," she said. "Masks could be made and we could use padding to protect bodies. And, of course, we have the emergency sacs."

The last resort, should a vessel be destroyed while in space, but only the insanely optimistic would ever use them. Transparent membranes containing air and other supplies which could maintain life for awhile; bubbles drifting in the void with those inside them, hoping against hope that some nearby vessel would hear their radio beacon and come to the rescue. The wise chose to die with their ship.

"The sacs!" The mercenary lifted his head like a dog smelling food. "The beacon—don't you have one fitted to the *Entil*?"

"Or a radio?" Roster added his suggestion. "We are on a listed world and it must have a field and people of some kind. We could contact them. Ask for rescue."

At a price which would leave them stripped of all assets but, dead, they would have lost everything anyway.

Zeda mistook Egulus's hesitation. "The radio, man! Are you afraid of losing your vessel as salvage?"

"It's lost anyway," said the captain. "But the radio's useless."

"And the beacon?"

Jumoke had overlooked it, as had Dumarest and the captain, both assuming the navigator had done his worst. Dilys sucked in her breath as she drew it from its housing; a small, compact piece of electronic wizardry which operated only when the generator failed and the field collapsed, sending a coded electronic "shout" which, even in the Rift, could be heard by a ship which was close, or by a nearby world. Even in the Quillian Sector.

And the thing had operated twice.

"A line," said Dilys. "If anyone heard both signals they could draw a line, extend it, and know just where we are."

"They won't be able to see us," said Egulus. "They could come looking and pass right over us."

But they would keep looking. A ship in distress was a fortune in salvage. Add to that the price of cargo, rescue fees and rewards, and no captain of a hungry trader would give up too soon.

And neither, Dumarest knew, would others who must be searching for him.

He said, "What now?"

"We wait." Bochner joined the discussion. "We sit and wait until someone comes to help us. Why not? We have air and food and water. We have wine and certain other comforts." He glanced at Gale Andrel. "So why risk death outside?"

"Perhaps we could rig up a new radio?" suggested Charl Zeda. "I've some experience in electronics and, with the emergency beacon intact, we have a viable base on which to build. And it doesn't have to be an ultra-radio—all we want is something which can contact someone locally and serve to guide them to us. You'll help me, Shan?"

"You need help?"

"For the assembly, yes." The mercenary gestured at his damaged shoulder. "I'm not too good at fine work at the best of times, and you're accustomed to handling delicate fabrications. If we could use the facilities in the engine room?"

"Sure," said Dilys. "Why not? I'll even—" She broke off

with a catch of breath. "What—what's that? What the hell's happening?"

The ship had moved.

It rolled a little, lifting to settle again, bumping to rest, to roll once more as, from the hull, came an ugly grating. A sound as if something hard had dragged over the metal. As the sound faded into silence, Gale said, "God, what's that?"

The screens answered her. In them loomed the shape of madness, scaled, tentacular, spines tipped with barbs, mouths lined with rows of savage teeth. A monstrous creature of the depths attracted by the shock of their landing, now busy investigating the intruder into its realm. And it was big. Big.

"It's like a mountain," whispered Fele Roster. With the others, he stood crammed into the control room and his whisper was an automatic defense mechanism; what the thing couldn't hear it couldn't be aware of. "A living mountain."

One which spread in formless confusion, fogging at the edge of visibility, coils writhing in seemingly endless profusion, tentacles filling its watery world. The *Entil* rolled like an egg in its grip, its bottom lifting to bang against the rocky bottom, to send metallic verberations echoing from the stricken metal, gongs to herald doom.

"The hull." Threnond's voice, while controlled, betrayed his strain. "How thick is it?"

"God knows." Egulus was somber. "We lost a lot of metal by vaporization as we came down. Half the thickness, and maybe more." He remembered the streaming incandescence which had accompanied them during their desperate journey through the atmosphere. Glowing gases born of disrupted molecules, the metal of the hull converted to light and heat by the friction of their descent. "But it'll hold."

A conviction Dumarest didn't share. He examined the screens and the thing they revealed, following lines, guessing as to size and mass. The ship, engulfed, would be small in comparison. The thing could lift it and slam it down until it broke. Or it could wait, maintaining the pressure of its grip until the hull yielded.

"We could seal the various compartments," said Gale Andrel. "But no, we have no way of telling which will go first."

"We could"—Dilys broke off, then appealed to the one

man she felt confident had the answer which could save their lives. "Earl—what should we do?"

Dumarest made no comment, looking at the interior of the vessel, moving from the control room to the greater spaciousness of the salon. Space ships were not built to operate as submarines. Strength of hull was not as important in the void as it would have been at great depths, but the fabric itself was strong to endure the strains and stresses of electronic storms and the warping effect of the Erhaft field. Strength, which meant weight. Struts and stanchions fitted on a geometric pattern so as to make the entire vessel an integrated unit. The immediate danger wasn't in crushing, but in the weakened hull plates yielding to admit the rush of water. A flood which would drown them like rats in a trap.

"Earl?"

"We can wait," he said. "Hope that the thing will tire and leave us before it manages to crack us open. But that's a gamble I prefer not to take."

"Why not?"

"Sound." Dumarest looked at Bochner, wondering why he had asked the question. Surely a hunter would know? "We move and hit things and talk. Vibrations transmitted through the fabric to the hull where that thing can sense them. It must know we aren't inanimate and, if it follows the usual pattern, it will be unwilling to give up its search for food."

"True." Bochner nodded. "What then?"

"We can try to sneak out and hope it won't follow us because we're so relatively small. You recommend that?"

"No. A thing that size will have attendant predators; scavengers living on its discards. They'd take care of us if the big beast didn't."

Gale Andrel said bitterly, "So that's it. We can't wait and we can't leave. Brilliant!"

"And defeatist." Bochner didn't look at her as he spoke. "There is an alternative."

"What?"

"We lighten the ship," said Dumarest. "We cut free and dump everything we can. The more we feed through the locks the greater our buoyancy will be. Once that thing out there releases its grip, we'll shoot up to the surface like a bubble."

"Simple," she said bitterly. "You make it sound all so

damned simple. But how are you going to make that thing
out there let us go?"

The air stank of burning, of hot metal which had vented
acrid vapors and coated the interior of the ship with noxious
patinas. Bright stubs showed where lastorches had burned
away installations, their energy adding to the trapped heat so
that a coating of moisture dewed the hull. An omen
Dumarest chose to ignore.

He stood in the control room, now such by courtesy only,
the chairs gone, the instruments, the delicate components
which had cost high but which had been discarded as so
much unwanted scrap. Only the screens remained alive, and
the communication link to the engine room.

"Now?" Egulus eased the collar of his uniform. His hands
were burned, sore, grimed, as was his face and hair, but
despite the heat, he clung to the symbols of his rank. He was
a captain and intended to remain one. "Earl?"

"A moment." Dumarest spoke into the intercom. "Dilys,
have Bochner vent the last of the material through port
four." He waited then, "Good. It's still clear. Now have Allain's body out in the final load and stand by for release."

The final load and a hell of a way to treat the dead,
though Egulus. To use them as bait. As a diversion. As a
bribe to the thing out there which still held them fast. The
dancer and historian didn't matter—those who hugged dirt
belong to it, but Allain had spent too many years in space to
be denied the clean expanse of the universe for his final
resting place.

Well—such things happened.

"You think it will work?"

"On its own? Probably not." Dumarest didn't take his eyes
from the screen. "I noticed a reaction when we dumped out
the stores. A tentacle went to investigate. It didn't return to
take up its old position. I think we've confused it a little, but
not enough to frighten it."

"Can such a thing feel fear?"

"Concern as to its survival, certainly. All living things must
feel that." Dumarest spoke into the intercom. "Dilys, how is
the potential? Optimum? Good. Maintain and stand by to dis-
charge." To the captain, he said, "Check that everyone is in-
sulated. No contact with metal of any kind."

Checking took less than a minute. With the interior of the ship now an almost empty shell, it was easy to spot those who waited.

"All clear and set, Earl."

Dumarest nodded, checked that he stood on a thick pad of wadded insulation, and said, "Right, Dilys. Give the word to Bochner. As soon as he's cycled out the load, hit the switches."

He stood, waiting, feeling the slight vibration of the cycling port, seeing the creature outside shift a little, a coil rippling as it moved, a gaping mouth snapping, a tentacle reaching to where the dead were floating up towards the surface.

Meat and blood and bone. Protein for the beast and for its attendant scavengers. Food they couldn't resist.

The coils moved faster then. As Dilys hit the switches, they jerked as if touched by redhot steel.

Current fed from the engines turned the hull into a searing, charring inferno. Tough skin and gristle burned, crisped, shed a sickly green ooze. Sparks flashed, as steam bubbled from the points of contact, lighting the screen with transient glimmers. More sparks flashed from within the ship itself. Streamers of manmade lightning, which added to the stench with its reek of ozone, sent tingles to jerk at nerve and muscle even through the wadded insulation.

The *Entil* lifted.

It rose, tilted, moved to halt again as, in a savage paroxysm, the tentacles gripped in self-destructive fury.

"Dilys!"

The power flow was at optimum, higher and it would threaten the source of its own creation, but as metal yielded, Dumarest knew the risk had to be taken.

"Maximum, Dilys! Feed every erg you can raise into the hull!"

A plate had bulged inward, another followed, water edging a crack, turning into a fine jet which sent spray lifting, to fall like rain. Rain which acted as a conductor for the electronic power so that arcs flashed and metal turned molten at the points of impact.

"Earl, for God's sake!" Egulus caught at his arm. "We're not going to make it!"

A statement punctuated by Gale Andrel's scream as Fele Roster, staggering, fell to touch the bare metal of the hull—

to turn into a pillar of smoking flesh, blood and charred bone.

A sacrifice which toppled to fall and lie sprawled on the floor as the ship lanced upwards.

To reach the surface and to rise above it. To hang suspended for a brief moment before crashing down. To sink and rise again and to roll sickeningly in the grip of crosscurrents and a screaming wind.

"We've got to get out!" Charl Zeda, his face gray with pain, stood in the opening of the control room. "Water's coming in."

Not enough to provide an immediate threat, but enough to send a shallow lake surging over the deck. Dilys came wading through it. Power was cut, the ship dark except for the pale glow of emergencies, shadows which held both real and imagined terrors.

"Earl?"

"We've got to abandon the ship." He staggered as the vessel rolled, landing hard against the hull, hearing the others shout and thresh in the water. "Get the emergency supplies and what extra clothing you reserved. The caskets—" He grunted as the ship rolled again. "I'll handle those with Bochner. Take care of the others, Captain. Keep them together."

Bochner was waiting at the main lock. Like Dumarest, he had changed into more serviceable clothing, thick materials, quilted and set with metal protection. He smiled at the tall figure in gray, his eyes flashing, noting the boots, the knife.

"A chance, Earl. The creature could be down there waiting for us."

"We've no choice."

"True, and if we stay too long we'll sink for the last time. But, honestly now, did you anticipate the need to abandon the ship?"

Dumarest said, "On the way down I noticed the wind. Without a keel, we were bound to roll with the impact. We have no rudder, no sails, nothing to enable us to steer a course. We could drift for months if we hadn't been broached."

"And now we have no choice at all." The hunter shrugged. "Well, so often it happens in life. The path one must follow is seldom the one offering the greatest delights. The caskets first?"

They slid from the port into the waves, the boxes sealed, bobbing, parting to the thrust of the wind. It droned over the sea, catching the leaden water, dashing waves against the wallowing hull. Bundles followed, all tightly wrapped and fitted with empty containers to ensure they would float. Then the survivors, Varn Egulus first.

He dived, surfaced, climbed on one of the caskets. Ropes had been attached and he gathered others to draw the containers close together.

Then Threnond, together with the mercenary, the latter sinking, to rise blowing and puffing, to sink again as his sore shoulder hampered his progress.

Beside him, something broke the water.

"Earl!" Dilys was beside him, her fingers digging into his arm. "That thing!"

A long, narrow shape, which glided like an oiled dart toward the struggling man. One with a long, needlelike jaw which gaped to reveal the flash of pointed teeth. The mercenary saw it, threshed, yelled as it swung in and away. Blood rose to stain the water with a carmine flood.

"Charl!" Threnond yelled from the safety of a casket. "Charl!"

He shouted at the wind.

"My God!" Gale lifted a trembling hand to her lips as she stared at where the mercenary had vanished. "What happened to him?"

"He's dead." Bochner was coldly dispassionate. "That predator must have got his leg. Those jaws could have severed the limb, and if they did, it would account for the amount of blood. Only ripped arteries could have produced so much so fast."

Dilys shuddered.

"But we are left with a problem," continued the hunter. "The blood will have attracted others and we have still to leave the ship." He glanced to where the caskets bobbed, together now in the form of a crude raft. "And our means of escape is moving further away."

Too far. Driven by the wind, the distance was increasing and those aboard had no way to return.

"We need a line." Dumarest turned, found an end of wire hanging from a conduit and ripped it from its housing. Lashing one end around his waist, he threw the other at Bochner. "Hold this. Give me slack. When it's fast to the raft, pull!"

"Earl!" Dilys stepped toward him, hands outstretched to hold him back. "No! You can't!"

She was too late. Even as she spoke he dived, hitting the water cleanly, vanishing to reappear swimming strongly through the waves. He had covered half the distance to the raft when the shape appeared.

The predator returned, or another just like it. A creature hungry for the kill.

Dumarest heard Bochner's warning shout and dived as it closed in, reaching for his boot, his knife. Steel glimmered in the water as he turned, eyes searching the gloom, seeing the long, slender body lance toward him, the jaws gaping, the expanse of the mottled belly as the creature closed in. A kick, and he moved aside just in time, the lower jaw rasping against his hip as, twisting, he plunged the blade into the exposed stomach, dragging back the steel in a long, deep cut which spilled blood and intestines in a fuming cloud.

The blade clamped between his teeth, Dumarest kicked himself to the surface and covered the rest of the distance to the caskets. Egulus reached down and hauled him to safety as water threshed and jaws snapped at the water where he had been.

"The line." Dumarest handed it to the captain. "Fasten it and pull. Hurry!"

It tightened, humming like a bowstring as the distance lessened between the ship and the crude raft. They touched as the *Entil* rolled, settled deeper as they watched, rolled again with a slow, deliberate movement.

"Jump!" Dumarest reached out to the open port as it swung down toward the waves. "Jump, damn you!"

Gale landed beside him, slipped and almost fell back into the water, steadied as his hands closed about her arms. Bochner thrust Dilys forward and she landed with surprising lightness for her size. The hunter followed, standing poised as the wind carried them away from the foundering vessel, watching as it tilted, the nose lifting, lowering, bubbles rising around it as, with sudden abruptness, it sank beneath the surface.

"Close." Egulus looked at the ring of spreading froth. "The hull must have given way after I'd left."

"It did." Bochner drew air deep into his lungs. His face was wet with spray and the wind turned his hair into a living crest. "Another few minutes and we'd have been food for the fish. Well, Earl, what now?"

"We lash everything tight, set up a sail and run before the wind." Dumarest looked at the sky, the seething spume rising from the waves, the clouds massed low on the horizon. The sun was a smeared copper ball, ringed with a lambent corona and blotched with ebon markings. The air held an acrid, metallic taint and, low on the horizon, he could see the dancing flicker of lightning. "And we'd better do it before the storm breaks."

Chapter Nine

The weather peaked at dusk, a hammer of wind racing over the ocean, lifting waves, filling the air with a screaming fury as lightning danced a jagged saraband. Filagrees of eye-searing brilliance reached from water to sky, the roar of thunder a savage accompaniment to the voice of the wind.

Lying huddled in her casket, Dilys Edhessa imagined herself to be dead and in hell.

It was ridiculous even to hope that anything could live through such a storm, and so the fact that she could breathe and hear and feel was nothing but an illusion—a part of the punishment meted out to those who had strayed from the path, or so the Elder had so often told her when she had attended the Place of Contemplation when a child.

A long time ago now, but she had never forgotten and now it was all present in sharp clarity; the old, musty building, the smell of hay and manure, the dampness, the hard benches, the cold impact of the floor against her knees. The dimness. The enigmatic shapes. The monotonous drone of the Elder, who stood fiercely proud of his power and authority and urged them all to be humble and obedient and true servants of the Revealed Truth. A bad time, and one she remembered only in nightmares. But she was dead and not asleep, so why should she be dreaming of the harsh time of childhood?

"Dilys!"

She felt the touch and stirred and looked up into Dumarest's face. And that, too, seemed a dream because he was leaning over her, head thrust into a narrow opening, water running down his hair and face and, behind him, the night blazed with unrestrained violence.

"Dilys!" His hand reached out to slap her cheek. "Wake up, girl! Wake up!"

"Earl?" Water gushed through the opening and she gasped in sudden shock. Abruptly awake, she became aware of the heaving of her chest, the pounding of her heart. "I was asleep, I think. Dreaming. I—"

"You were dying." His voice was harsh with anger. "You kept the lid sealed too long and were breathing your own carbon dioxide."

A mistake both Egulus and Threnond had made as they shared a casket, but which Bochner had not. He had helped to check the lashings and adjust the tattered fabric used as a sail. He had even laughed into the fury of the storm.

"An experience to remember, my friend. At least, the weather is keeping the predators below. Now, if we can remain afloat—"

If the caskets held and the lashing kept them together. If the lightning missed and no rocks waited to rip them open with jagged teeth. If they could run before the wind and not drown or suffocate in their containers then, possibly, they might survive to drift in calm waters. But not yet.

Dilys gasped as Dumarest eased himself into the casket beside her. His clothing was glistening with water and his hands bore thin, ugly welts from the stranded wire used to lash the caskets together. When they were settled close, she said, "Is everything all right?"

"So far, yes."

"You were out there a long time."

Almost too long. He remembered her pallor, the waxen appearance of her face which had given her the likeness of a corpse. A big woman, she needed a lot of oxygen to maintain the fires of her body. He had warned her to keep the lid cracked so as to admit air but she had forgotten, or had been already numbed by inhaling the waste product of her lungs.

Now, shivering, she said, "The water's cold, Earl. So very cold."

"It'll be warm soon."

"I was dreaming," she said, "of when I was young. I came from a stern culture, Earl. Did I tell you that? A farming community which tried to follow the Revealed Truth. We used no machinery of any kind. Nothing but natural fertilizers. No energy other than that provided by natural means—muscles and the use of ropes and levers. Of pulleys and wheels."

"Machinery."

"No, Earl. Such things were not considered to be that. We used no artificial means of power, but we had a windmill and a water wheel and. . . ." She nodded, almost asleep, then jerked in his arms, gasping. "They killed a man. Stoned him to death. They tied him up by the wrists to a post and stood close and threw stones at him until he stopped screaming. Stopped moving. It was horrible!"

Another pause. Water blasted through the narrow crack and drenched her face and hair, and lightning blazed to hurl brilliance through the transparent lid. In its glare her lips looked black and her hair silver.

"Why?" Dumarest shook her. "Why did they kill him?"

"What?" She gasped again, her breasts pressing against his body, eyes blinking as they tried to focus. "The man? Why, he'd devised a system of mirrors to reflect the rays of the sun so as to heat water in a boiler and so produce steam. With it, he turned a painted wheel set with bright crystal. A toy to amuse the children, Earl. A toy—and they killed him because of it."

"For making a machine?"

"Yes," she said dully. "For making a machine."

"And the windmill and water wheel?"

"Were allowed under the Revealed Truth. The wind blew and the water flowed, but the sun did not boil water and to force it to do that was acting against the creed. It was to invite the seeds of destruction to cast down the race again."

Dumarest said quietly, "From terror, they fled to find new places on which to expiate their sins. Only when cleansed will the race of Man be again united."

The creed of the Original People—was Dilys one? Had she originated in a commune of the sect? Had the "Revealed Truth" she had mentioned contained the belief that all men had originated on one world and that world had been possibly Earth?

Terror—Terra.

An easy enough transition from one to the other and if she knew, she might, in her present state of mental fog induced by too high a percentage of carbon dioxide, be induced to betray the closely guarded secret.

"Earl?" She stared at him in puzzlement. "What did you say?"

"Nothing. It doesn't matter." A hope to be discarded along with so many others. More than one commune had turned their backs on machinery, and she had obviously been born into one. But, in that case, how had she become an engineer?

"The man who was stoned was my brother," she said, when he asked. "I had to do what I could to avenge him."

By leaving the community and doing the one thing they would have hated most for her to do; to embrace the vileness they condemned. To become a servant of the machine.

"Earl?"

"Nothing." He eased his arm around her, cushioning her against his body, against the punishing slap of the waves. "Go to sleep, now."

"You'll stay with me?" Like a child, she needed reassurance. "You'll take care of me?"

"Yes."

"You promise? Earl, you promise?"

"I promise."

She sighed and settled and fell asleep, with her lips parted and the soft mounds of her breasts rising to press against him like small, insistent hands. Lying beside her, he watched the glare of lightning tracing pictures in the sky. Spume thrown by the wind dashed against the lid like rain. Droplets which clung and quivered to the thrust of waves, which ran and formed patterns illuminated by the stroboscopic effect of the lightning.

Faces. Hair the color of flame, of ebon, of silver and of rich, warm brown earth. Eyes which held longing and tenderness, fear, anger and hate. A scarlet shape which advanced with extended hands ready to take and hold and bend the universe to its will. A ruby monster, squatting like a spider at the heart of a web of intrigue.

The fifteen units of the affinity twin.

Kalin's gift, and one which the Cyclan would spare no effort to recover. The discovery made in one of their secret laboratories, stolen, passed on, now his alone. The knowledge of the sequence in which the fifteen units must be assembled to be viable.

A secret which could give them the galaxy.

Thunder roared and the casket tilted, a fresh wave dashing

over the lid so that when the lightning next flared, the images had changed. But the sequence would never be lost until Dumarest was dead, or his mind so damaged as to be virtually destroyed.

The affinity twin—an artificial symbiont which, when injected into the bloodstream, moved to the base of the cortex, to nestle there, to take over control of the entire nervous and sensory apparatus of the body. An intruder, which would act as an organic relay, creating an affinity between the dominant half and the subject-host. An affinity which was a literal cojoining so that, in effect, the dominant half became the host, seeing, feeling, hearing, using all the motor and sensory apparatus.

An old and dying man could become young again in a new and virile body. A cripple become whole. A beggar become a ruler. A crone look into the mirror and see a beauty. And all would keep their new shapes until they died, or their own body failed.

Power of incredible potential locked in the arrangement of fifteen units.

The Cyclan knew it, and knew how to use it. They would place the mind of a cyber into the body of every ruler and person of influence, and all would dance to their dictates. But before they could hope for that power, they had to find the order of assembly. They were trying. They would continue to try, but mathematics was against them. The possible combinations ran into millions, and it took time to assemble and test them all. Too much time. Millenia would be needed to check them all.

Time the Cyclan wanted to save.

Time he could save them. Time . . . time . . . time . . .

Dumarest woke, gasping, reaching up and lifting the lid, relishing the cool breeze clearing the stale air from the casket. It was a new day and the storm had passed, the container drifting on an even plane in the water, barely rocking to the slap of waves. Easing himself from the woman's arms, he threw back the lid and rose, breathing deeply the clear, crisp air.

"Earl!" Leo Bochner was up and sitting on the casket he shared with Gale Andrel. "I was just about to call you."

"Why?"

"Look around. We're in trouble."

The sail was still with them, a tattered fragment flapping against the mast they had fashioned from welded pipe. The buoyancy containers rode snug in their frayed lashings, but of the four caskets they had started with only three remained. One had vanished during the night. With it had gone their water and food.

Shen Threnond adjusted the sheet of plastic and, as it bellied with the wind, said, "Once, on Sante, I saw a man who had fasted for thirty days. It was a show at a carnival and I think he was doing it for a bet. If he lasted for thirty-seven days he would have beaten the record."

Egulus said, "Did he?"

"I don't know. I moved on before the period ended but I am sure he did. He seemed fit enough when I saw him. A little spare, perhaps, but fit."

"Going without a few meals doesn't hurt anyone." Bochner looked up from his work. "I've starved for days at a time when on a stalk, and gained because of it. Hunger sharpens the senses and cleanses the body. Of course, some can do without better than others."

Gale Andrel snapped, "Meaning me, I suppose. Hell, can't you talk about anything but food? I'm starving!"

"Not starving," he corrected. "You just want to eat. You're not even really hungry yet. It's just that your stomach is accustomed to be filled at regular intervals and has started to complain. Just be patient. In a few days, it will pass."

Less than that. They had drifted for two days since the storm had ended, but food wasn't the major problem. Thirst would kill them long before they could starve.

Dumarest spread the flotation container he had cut open, set it with others and glanced at Bochner.

"Finished yet?"

"Almost." The hunter, too, had a knife, a heavy-bladed instrument with a serrated back which could saw through bone. With it, he had cut thin metal into strips and had rolled them into a spiral tube. Plastic cut from a sheet had sealed the joins. "Here."

Taking it, Dumarest set one end into a water-filled container set within the ring of curved metal plates. The other end he sealed within a plastic bag, which he suspended in the sea.

"Some distillery." Dilys shook her head as she studied it. "Where did you get the idea of using focused sunlight to heat the boiler?"

"From you."

"You did?" She blinked, not remembering. "Well, even if it works, the output will be low."

But better than nothing, and it gave them something to do. Egulus and Gale could attend it while Threnond busied himself with his radio. And Dilys, as engineer, had been put in charge of the raft itself.

Now, looking over the ocean, she said, "How long can we last, Earl? I mean really last. I can take the truth even if others can't."

By the movement of her eyes, he knew she meant the other woman.

"We can last as long as we want to."

"On hope?"

"On work. On resolve. You know what keeps people alive? The desire to live. The determination. Too many give up too quickly. They defeat themselves. They wait for help and when none arrives, they give up." Dumarest pointed at the sea. "Look at it. A place full of water and food."

"Food?"

"Fish, girl. Fish."

"If we can catch them. But water?"

"In the fish." He smiled at her blank expression. "Didn't you know that? A fish is full of drinkable water. All you need to do is catch one, cut it open, scrape it to a pulp and eat it."

"Is that all?" She remembered the thing which had almost killed him and which had killed Charl Zeda. "And if it has other ideas?"

"We change its mind." He dropped his hand on her shoulder. "Make me a line and hooks—you'll have to use wire and what metal is available. And something for bait. Bright rag, or something shiny might do to snare our first catch. After that, we can use the body for bait."

Bochner shook his head as he came close. Then, at Dumarest's side, he said softly, "Spacers—what do they know about basic survival? And if you think catching fish is so easy, why all the work on the distillery?"

"You tell me."

"Insurance. You alone, or with one other, could survive

with comparative ease. But six of us? No, Earl, not while we're all cramped on this raft. Small fish won't have enough water content to satisfy us all, and if we attract larger specimens, then it will be us, not they, who will provide the repast." Bochner glanced at the sun. "Hot," he mused. "We're going to sweat. A matter of days, I think. Even with fish, a matter of days. Then the trouble will start."

The quarrels, the stealing, the fighting, the apathy and, perhaps, the murders. Certainly the deaths. Who would be the first to go? Threnond was old, but his frame was tough, and in his time he had lived hard. Bochner glanced to where he sat in one of the caskets, busy with his radio. Egulus? Also tough, but with a different form of hardness. Space weakened a man for survival in the wild. Dilys? She was big and so would lose more water because of her larger surface area, but she would have a good reserve of fat and Dumarest would certainly help her all he could. Gale Andrel? Small, compact, light-boned but with scant fat, and accustomed to civilized ease. Already, she had begun to complain.

She would be the first to die.

They would all die unless they reached shore soon, or help arrived, and to hope for that was to believe in miracles. Caradoc was on Mucianus, waiting for the *Entil* to arrive. Trusting in the traps and snares, the arranged cargoes which were to have guided it there, himself to see that Dumarest was on it when it did. A good plan negated by a fool. How long would the cyber wait? Not long, Bochner knew, then Caradoc would go hunting. With luck, he would discover the emergency signals from the *Entil*. With his trained skill, he might even be able to determine which world they had reached.

And then?

Bochner smiled and stretched his legs and watched Dumarest at his work. The quarry, tracked and now ready at hand, the stalk over and the sport ended before it had really begun. A disappointment. But a question remained: Why did the Cyclan want Dumarest so badly? What did he know or possess which made him so valuable?

To discover that would be to engage in a hunt of another kind and the reward, once the kill was made, could be incredible.

It was taking too long.

Death should not come on slow, creeping feet, but be mercifully swift so that, at the end, there was no pain, not even the anticipation of hurt but a sudden, devastating extinction. There shouldn't be endless days in which the sun burned like a furnace in a mottled sky, and heat radiated from the water, the caskets, the sail itself as it flapped against the mast. Only the nights were kind, the heavens blazing with a luminous splendor reflected in the ocean, the image broken, at times, by leaping shapes, ripples spreading to reach to infinity.

Gale Andrel looked at it, her back against the mast, salt crusting her hair from where she had plunged her head into the sea. Salt which stung her lips and eyes, creating tears which added to the illusion.

Light, winking and shimmering, forming patterns which changed, turning sea and sky into a mirrored image, an intricate chiaroscuro of silver and black which swelled to embrace her, to engulf her, to swallow her in its insatiable mouth.

Death wore beauty as a garment.

But death came accompanied by pain.

Thirst consumed her, a fire which could not be quenched. Her lips were cracked, her throat constricted, every cell and fiber yearning for water. Pools, baths, rivers into which she could plunge. Waterfalls and cascades of icy coldness. Long drinks in dew-adorned glasses, tart and heavy with the chill of ice.

She needed to drink. She had to drink—and if death followed, then it was worth the price.

Lying on the casket, stripped, body glistening with perspiration, Bochner saw her move and said nothing. On another, Dilys, restless, lifted herself on one elbow; a near-naked shape occluding the stars. Wakened by her movement, Dumarest whispered, "Dilys?"

"It's Gale. She—" Her voice rose to a shout. "No, you fool! No!"

Dumarest heard the splash as he rose. Like the others, he was naked but for shorts, hard white flesh gleaming in the starlight, silver droplets lifting as he plunged after the girl who now floated in the sea. Bochner caught him as he reached the edge of the raft.

"No!"

"The girl—"

"She's mad. Thirst-crazed. Gulping down sea water even as she bathes in it." He grunted as Dumarest pushed him aside. "No, you fool! The predators—"

They had followed for days, eager for the prey they sensed would inevitably be theirs. Long shapes which glided, breaking water at times, never coming too close to risk capture, ignoring the baited hooks which had only caught their natural prey sheltering under the raft. Now, as the girl thrashed in wild abandon, they closed in.

Dumarest saw them as he stood, knife in hand, eyes calculating time and distance. A moment, then he dived, hitting the water in a shallow curve, reaching the girl to grab her by the hair, to drag back her face, to slam his knife-weighted fist hard against her jaw. As he headed back to the edge of the raft, the first predator struck.

Dazed, half-stunned by the blow which had forestalled her anticipated resistance, the girl felt the rasp of scales against her thighs and screamed.

"Earl!" Bochner stood on the edge of the raft, hand extended. "Quickly, you fool! Quickly!"

"The girl—"

"To hell with her." The hunter snarled his impatience. "Save yourself, man. Hurry!"

He snarled again as Dumarest ignored the instruction and dived in turn. He hit the water like an eel, twisting, body curved, hand and knife extended as, again, the predator attacked. Blood foamed from the creature, to fog the water and dull the gleam of starlight. More blood followed as the girl screamed. Dumarest released her, slashed at an arrowing shape, felt the impact of his blade on skin and flesh.

"Gale!"

She drifted to one side, face down, hair spread, cradled in the water as beneath her something rose to tear, to sink again.

"Earl!" Bochner thrashed at the water, then headed toward the raft. "Quick, man. The girl's dead. Save yourself!"

Move while the girl provided a distraction. Reach the raft while her body was being torn into shreds. To grip outstretched hands and to climb to safety. To slump, conscious of weakness, of the price exertion needed to be paid.

"Earl!" Dilys was beside him, her face anxious as she

stared at his thigh, the raw patch where the skin had been rasped and which now oozed blood. "You're hurt!"

"I'll live."

"Gale—"

"Is dead." Hadn't she seen? "We can't help her now, but we can help ourselves. Let's get some of those fish!"

Crazed by the blood, the flesh, the fish were easy prey to the nooses, the lines and hooks, the stabbing blades. Before they dispersed, three of them jerked in one of the caskets adding their blood to the saline in which they died. Food and water for those who survived—the gift Gale Andrel had bought with her life.

"She was crazed," said Bochner dispassionately. "I guessed she'd be the first to go. I knew she was near the edge, but didn't think she was about to break."

"You should have stopped her."

"Going into the sea? How?" The hunter stared at Dilys. "She was gone before I knew it, and once in the water what could I have done?"

"What Earl did. Gone in after her."

"And got myself killed as he almost did?" Bochner pointed to the wound. "If I hadn't gone in after him when I did, that leg wouldn't be scraped, it'd be gone. He'd be dead now, if it hadn't been for me."

A claim Dumarest didn't bother to dispute, but why had the man dived into the sea to help him and not the girl?

Egulus said, "I think the wind is rising. Look at the sail."

It billowed from the mast, snapping, suddenly taut, and the captain went to adjust one of the guy ropes. When it was to his satisfaction he stood, looking upwards, starlight limning his face, his eyes. An aged and haggard face. A pair of yearning eyes.

Dumarest could understand why. Up there, in the vast immensities of space, ships lanced from world to world, eating distance with the power of their drives, while down where the captain stood, they inched along over endless water on a bleak journey to an unknown destination.

He said quietly, "It won't be long before you're back up there, Captain."

"As what?" Egulus didn't lower his eyes. "A steward? A handler? What chance have I of ever getting another ship of my own?"

"The big lines?"

"Don't want or trust men who've been free traders. We're too independent, and not used to wearing the reins. Once a man's had a ship of his own—" Egulus sighed and looked down and became suddenly brusque. "To hell with it! Let's get busy on these damned fish before the sun rises to bake our bones!"

The next day they saw land.

Chapter Ten

It loomed on the horizon, a smudge against the harsh clarity of the sky, a blur which gradually gained resolution. A high peak, flanked by lesser hills, all joined by a series of slopes which ran down to a shore of black, volcanic sand, toothed with rocks against which the sea lashed in foaming irritation.

In pools, they found limpets and mollusks which provided a mouthful of moist nourishment—the fish they had caught had been consumed in the three days they had waited to be carried to land. Edging the shore, vegetation rose in a dull, green wall, boles darkly brown against the sand, the leaves spined and serrated like the blades of vicious spears.

"There could be a break," suggested Egulus. "If we follow the coast, we could find a river or something."

"We need water, food and shelter," said Dumarest. "We won't find them by hugging the shore."

"But can we move through that tangle?" Dilys touched a leaf, moved it to one side, looked at the web of branches waiting in the gloom. "We'll be cut to shreds."

"Not if we take precautions." Dumarest glanced at the raft. It held materials which could be fashioned into forms of protection. "We've got clothing and can use extra padding. Get ready, now. Wear all you can, and make sure you protect face and hands." His voice hardened as only Bochner made a move. "Do it, damn you! If you hope to live, get to work!"

Bochner had his quilted and protected garb, as Dumarest had his own clothing. With thick gloves, crudely shaped but serviceable, and with heads enclosed in metal cans cut with slits to provide vision, they moved to take the lead. The vegetation was stubborn, falling slowly beneath their knives, the metal edges blunting and showing the stains of acid.

"We need lasers," grumbled the hunter. "Heavy-duty weapons to burn a path through this jungle. With knives alone, we haven't a chance."

"It should thin further within." Dumarest rasped the side of a stone over his blade. "We'll take turns, me, then you, then me, again. Short spells and halt to sharpen. A narrow passage will do as long as the branches are cut to allow progress. We'll halt to rest when we reach a clearing."

It took three hours during which they hacked and cut and squeezed past ripping thorns and jagged spines, their padding torn, sweat running down their bodies, the roar of blood loud in their ears as they sagged from exhaustion.

Dilys collapsed as they reached the clearing, lying to gasp, to pull the fabric from head and face, to sprawl, panting like a dog. Threnond was little better. Egulus leaned back against a mass of branches and looked upwards. The sky was hidden beneath a roof of greenery.

"Food," he said bitterly. "Water and shelter. Well, I guess we've found that, at least. The shelter of a grave. We could die in here and no one would ever be able to find us."

"If anyone is bothering to look." Bochner looked up from where he sat. "Any luck with the radio yet?"

"I've been sending a distress call for days, now." Threnond looked at the radio equipment in his hand. It was a jumble of adapted components, powered by a small energy cell. "If anyone's heard it, they haven't answered."

"Or you haven't caught it, if they did." Egulus was pessimistic. "What difference does it make? They'll never find us in here."

"Not here," agreed Dumarest, "but we'd be easy to spot if we were on the summit of that peak we saw."

"The peak?" Dilys lifted her head. "Earl, that's miles away! We can't—"

"We can!" He rose and stepped toward her and lifted her upright with an explosion of violence which gave his face the likeness of a savage animal. "We can if we try. If we want to. But we won't if we just sit around moaning that it can't be done. Now, move! On your feet and move!"

The sun passed zenith and headed toward the horizon. An hour before dusk they found a small stream and bathed, cooling their bodies and filling their stomachs in turn, as others kept watch; a precaution Dumarest insisted on and one which Bochner noted. A trait of his quarry's character—how many would have thought to be so careful at such a time and in such a seemingly harmless place?

Later, as the shadows closed in, he said, "We need to eat, Earl. Climbing to that peak will take energy the rest haven't got. Of course, we could leave them here and send help later."

Or forget them. The simplest way, but he didn't hint at that. The bait had been enough. He could learn from the way it was taken.

"We could," said Dumarest, "if we find help. If that help is willing to do as we ask. If it can find them when it tries."

"An old man," said Bochner. "A captain without a ship. A woman."

"People."

"True, but there are so many people." Bochner looked into the shadows. "With water there could be game. If so, it would follow trails—need I tell you what is obvious?"

They set snares made of woven wires and waited and caught small, furred creatures which squeaked and died and were skinned to roast over a fire created by sparks struck from steel. Daylight provided more food from the snares which had been set overnight, and again they began to climb. At dusk, the vegetation had developed into tall trees which soared like the columns of an ancient cathedral, their upper branches plumed to hide the sky. Progress was easier, but slowed by the thick humus which held the damp consistency of mud.

And there was no more game.

Its lack puzzled Bochner.

"There are fruits," he pointed out. "And there should be things to eat them. There are insects and yet no apparent lifeform adapted to prey on them. See?"

With his boot he scraped back a portion of the dirt, revealing a host of scurrying beetles. The fruits, small, hard-skinned, now rotting, lay where they had fallen.

Dumarest looked at the trees, the immediate area. Life took many forms, but always it followed certain patterns. The large preyed on the small and where there was food there was something to eat it. The animals they had snared and eaten had been rodents, ratlike things with teeth and jaws adapted to an omnivorous diet. They had been fairly plentiful further down the slopes—why not here?

Threnond said, "What's the matter? Are we lost?"

"No."

"How can you tell?" The dealer in items of death was hungry and irritable and conscious of his overriding fatigue. He set down the radio and moved off into the shadows clustered between the boles. "While you decide, I've something to attend to. A natural function—you understand."

A delicacy he had demonstrated before, but not with such abruptness. Dumarest took a step after him, halted as Bochner rested a hand on his arm.

"Let him go, Earl."

"There could be danger."

"Always there is the possibility of danger, my friend. In the wine you drink, the food you eat, the bed in which you sleep. We are surrounded by perils, but to guard against them all is beyond the ability of man. We take what precautions we can and, for the rest, we trust to luck. If our luck is good, we continue to survive. If it is bad—" he shrugged, "then we cease to have cause to worry."

And no man should be fool enough to burden himself with the welfare of another—a point Bochner hadn't emphasized but had left in no doubt. A tenet of his philosophy revealed in the tone of his voice, the expression of his eyes, the words chosen to illustrate a meaning. When a man played cards, he betrayed more than he guessed to a skilled observer and Dumarest had assessed his motivation. The cult of self, the way of the feline. The law of the beast who has only one instinct, one drive. To survive at all costs. To live. To continue to exist, for without personal existence there was nothing.

And yet he had dived into the ocean, risking death to save another.

"Threnond!" Dumarest raised his voice. "Shan? Shan, where are you?"

Silence, broken only by the rustle of feet in the humus as the woman and Egulus came to join them. A silence which held a sudden, brooding menace.

"Shan!"

"He can't be far," whispered Dilys. "There was no need for him to go far."

"Shan!" Dumarest looked up and around, feeling the old, familiar prickle of impending danger, the primitive warning which had served him so well before. "Stay together," he said. "Keep watch. Bochner, you light a fire. Hurry!"

He moved to where a clump of saplings stood between separated trees. As flame rose from the fire the hunter had built, Dumarest cut down four of the slender poles, trimmed them, sharpened their ends to form crude spears.

As Dilys took hers, she said, "Why this, Earl? Trouble?"

"Maybe not. Just hold on to it, in case. Use it to lean on if you like."

"Sure, just like an—"

She broke off as he lifted a hand, listening. From above and to one side, falling with a gentle rustle through the leaves, came something which twisted and turned to land like a flattened snake.

"A belt!" Egulus lunged forward. "By God, it's a belt!"

After it came nightmare.

It dropped with a thin chatter of castanets, veiled, gems flashing in the firelight, fans and parasols flared and shimmering with a nacreous sheen. A thing which followed the bole, suspended on a thin strand, swinging, touching Egulus, who yelled and sprang back and yelled again as he fell, to roll helpless on loam.

To stare with horror at the mammoth spider dropping towards him.

"Earl! My God! What—"

Dilys spoke to empty air. Dumarest was gone, lunging forward with a speed which, in the firelight, made him seem little more than a blur. To halt, spear upraised, butt on the loam beside the fallen captain, the sharpened point buried deep in the mat of fur covering the spider's thorax, wood shredding beneath the snap of its mandibles, silk pluming from the pulsing spinnerets forming clouds of gossamer which drifted like a mantle to clog his head and arms.

A silken shroud from which he tore himself with desperate energy.

"Earl!" Bochner shouted from where he came running. "Above!"

A hint of movement in the shadows and another monstrous creature plumeted, to strike and seize and lift its prey to the

lair it owned high in the topmost branches of the trees.
Dumarest sprang aside, steel lifting from his boot, point and
edge cutting at the snapping castanets of the mandibles, stabbing at the gems of the eyes. Ichor dripped on his hand, and
an acrid stench filled his nostrils as hooked limbs tore shreds
from his padding. Limbs which jerked as they were slashed,
to lie severed on the loam, twitching as the body of the creature twisted on its suspending filament, to attack with
mindless ferocity again, to die as Bochner impaled it with his
wooden shaft.

"Back!" The hunter looked up. "Back, Earl! There could
be more!"

"Get to the girl!" Dumarest stooped, grabbed the captain
by the arms and dragged him upright to his feet. Bochner
hadn't moved. "Damn it, man! Get to the girl!"

A fraction of hesitation and the hunter obeyed. Dilys stood
beside the fire, eyes wide, spear trembling in her hand as she
stared into the shadows. From above, from all sides, came a
thin chittering, a scrape and rustle of chiton, the impact of
limbs against branches and leaves as things edged forward
through the upper layers of vegetation.

"A nightmare." Egulus looked ill. "A thing from hell itself.
It almost had me. It would have had me but for Earl.
Threnond?"

He hadn't been as lucky. Dumarest held out the belt he
had recovered, together with the spears.

"Is it his?"

"I don't know. It could have been." Egulus shivered.
"What now?"

"We build up the fire. Gather fuel—go with him, Bochner.
Keep guard while he picks up what he can."

"And me, Earl?"

"You stay here." He looked at the woman. "Keep the fire
as high as you can. Don't move away from it, but don't stay
immobile. Move about, look around, keep watch and if you
see anything, scream."

"And that will drive them away?"

"No." He was blunt. "But it may distract them."

"For how long?" She stared into the darkness, her voice
high, thin, verging on hysteria. "All right? And after that,
what? Can we stay awake all the time? Can we hope to beat
those things off as we move? Earl! What the hell can we do?"

"We wait," he said. "We watch and we plan. We keep our heads. Now tend the fire."

A job which would keep her busy and occupy her mind. Flames rose as she fed scraps of wood to the coals, leaping tongues of red and orange, edged with grayish smoke, the light painting the boles around with shimmers of transient brightness, glows which faded to flare again, to give the impression of movement, of watching eyes.

"They'll come again," said Bochner. "They've tasted blood and they'll be eager for more easy prey."

Egulus said, "Threnond—a hell of a way for a man to die. Squatting, thinking, then something swinging down to—" He broke off, swallowing. "He didn't even have time to scream. And then what? They lifted him up? Carried him? Held him in a web like a fly? Thank God, he knew nothing about it."

"Maybe," said Dumarest.

"He was dead," said Bochner quickly. "He had to be dead. Otherwise he would have screamed or struggled. We'd have heard something."

"We did."

"His belt falling. What does that mean?"

Dumarest said, "He wore that belt under his clothing, so to fall, it must have been exposed. Which means he was stripped."

"So where's the rest of his clothing?"

"I don't know," admitted Dumarest. "Maybe it was shredded and scattered around. Maybe it's up in the trees and the belt fell by accident."

"If it hadn't, I'd be dead by now," said Egulus. "We could all be dead." He looked up and around, eyes uneasy, a muscle twitching on one cheek. "For God's sake, can't we get away from here? Move back down the slope? Find a clearing or something?"

"Tomorrow, yes."

"Why not now?"

"We're trapped," said Bochner. "If we move away from the fire, they'll have us. If we try to take it with us, they'll follow. All we can do is to keep it alight and watch. If we're lucky, they won't attack in force."

"And if not?"

"We'll be dead." The hunter smiled. "We'll die fighting, but we'll be dead just the same. A brave finish, you agree? To

stand with companions battling hopeless odds. Sagas have
been written about less. But have hope, friend. Always have
hope."

Dumarest said, "They won't attack in force. If that was
their habit, we'd have been overrun long ago. I think it's a
matter of territory—game belongs to the spiders under whose
trees it strays. At the moment, we're at a junction, as it were,
and so present a problem. When the vacancy we made by
killing those things is filled, then the newcomers may attack."

Dilys said, "And if they do?"

"We fight back. We win."

"And leave?"

"Yes," said Dumarest. "After we have found Threnond."

Bochner stirred, not asleep yet not wholly awake, his mind
drifting in a vague region composed of memory and fantasy,
constructing regions of what-might-have-been together with
those of what-could-be. Dumarest was far more complex than
he had at first appeared. There were levels within the man
which he was only now beginning to fully appreciate. A sense
of function, of fitness, of instinctive reaction which added
new dimensions to apparent simplicity. Nothing he did could
be simple, always there had to be a complex motivation directed not even on a conscious level but operating on the subconscious need to ensure survival. And yet, there were
elements which negated that facile theory. A man driven by
the need simply to exist was predictable and so made poor
sport. Threaten, and he would respond in one of certain
ways; he would beg, run, bribe, plead, bargain, even kill.
Dumarest would do all these, if necessary, and yet that was
not all. There had to be more. If not, how had he managed
to elude the Cyclan for so long?

And what made them so desperate to find and hold him?

Always it came back to that—the tantalizing promise of
fantastic reward. Not just for the sake of material gain but
for the other, far more intense pleasure of personal achievement. Of running down the most wily and the most dangerous quarry he had ever known to the final, bitter end. Not
just to make a kill—any fool could destroy—but to win on
all levels so that when the hunt was ended, the stalk consum-
mated, and he was closing in for the termination, the usual
orgasmic pleasure would be multiplied a hundredfold.

To win.

To pit mind against mind, body against body, skill and cunning and intelligence against equal attributes and to win. To be proven the best. To gain in stature by the other's defeat.

To live!

A noise, and he was fully awake, one hand reaching for his knife, the other for his spear. Against the glow of the fire, the bulk of the woman showed monstrous; female flesh rendered even more shapeless by the clothing and padding she wore. For a moment he compared her with Gale Andrel and her slim boyishness, then dismissed them both. Women, never important, were now an unwanted complication.

Dumarest stood beyond her, head tilted, eyes searching the heights. Egulus, lying supine, stirred and coughed—the noise he had heard—and Bochner lifted himself from the loam to rise and flex his muscles. A creature of the wild preparing himself for action.

They had, he thought, been lucky. It was close to dawn and the night had passed without incident. Lying, resting his bones if nothing else, he had waited on the edge of instant alertness, ready for any attack, eyes acting as watchful guardians as, apparently, he dreamed. Now, with the new day, they could move back down the slope, skirt the area, press on up the hill to the peak.

If the area could be skirted.

If there was no attack.

Standing, he felt his mind flash to an alternate possibility. He and Dumarest, wandering this world, two hunters living on the land, knowing and relishing the taste and feel of a primitive existence, sharing and finding joy in their own, personal world.

A moment, then it was gone and only a semiregretful glow remained. The main hunt still remained. The stalk, the challenge, the need to act, to delude, to beat intelligence and caution with the same of his own.

He said, "Earl? Are we ready to move out?"

"Not yet." Dumarest, Bochner noticed, had removed all the padding he'd worn. "Strip. I want everything but your own clothing. You too, Dilys. And you, captain."

"Why?"

"For smoke. Most of the padding is plastic and it'll produce a thick, black cloud when burned."

"Smoke?" Egulus frowned, then thought he had the answer. "To get rid of the spiders? Will it work?"

"It might. At least, it will stop them seeing me."

"Seeing you?" Dilys remembered what he had said. "Earl, you're not going after Threnond!"

"Someone has to."

"But why? He's dead. You said so yourself."

"No, others said that. I'm afraid he could still be alive." Dumarest stooped and lifted burning sticks from the fire. "If he is, then he's in the worst kind of hell. We can't leave him in it."

He carried the mass of burning wood to the place where the belt had fallen and she followed him, searching for words, for a reason why he shouldn't do what he obviously intended to do. Only a madman would want to climb the tree to face what could lurk above. Threnond was dead—he had to be dead. How could he possibly be alive?"

Bochner knew. He said urgently, "Earl, the risk is too great. Even if they did sting and poison him, there's nothing you can do. We have no cure. You'd be throwing your life away for nothing."

Dumarest said, "If you want to help, stand guard while Dilys feeds the fire. If not, get the hell away from here. Captain?"

"I'm with you, Earl." Egulus came forward, his arms filled with discarded padding, eyes anxious as he stared into the dying night. "I don't understand this, but in space we help each other. Threnond wasn't a spacer, but he'd bought passage and I guess I'm responsible for him, in a way." He added with simple dignity, "Just tell me what you want me to do."

"Stand guard, keep watch, take care of anything which might attack." Dumarest glanced at the bole of the tree, his eyes following it to the summit. "It's light up there. Dilys, start making smoke."

It billowed from the embers as she fed plastic to the embers, thick, black, acrid. Rising in a pillar about the bole of the tree, drawn upwards by the dawn wind blowing over the forest, spreading in odd vagaries of shape, coils hanging as if solid, to writhe, to drift like reluctant phantoms, to stain the greenery with fingers of pollution.

In the midst of it, Dumarest climbed upwards like a mechanical doll. A rope circled the tree, the loop enclosing his body and forming a rest against which he could strain while his boots found holds on the trunk. Hands flapping the rope upwards, body moving in synchronization with feet and support, he was gone before they knew it, a dim shape which vanished into darkness.

"They'll get him," said Egulus. "He won't be able to see them and they'll get him before he knows it."

"No." Bochner released his breath in a long sigh. "He knows what he's doing. The smoke will clear the area."

Of spiders and oxygen, both given time. And the released poisons could be as fatal to man as arachnids. Why was he risking his life? Why?

High above, Dumarest paused, blinking, conscious of the pain in his lungs, the constriction. The cloth he had wrapped around his mouth did little to filter the smoke from the air and it was time to lose even that protection. A quick move and it was around his throat, the blade of his knife clamped in his mouth, and again he was climbing up to where the leaves made an umbrella to trap the smoke as it hid the sky.

The sky and other things.

Something thin and sticky touched his cheek, stinging, as he forged upwards and tore it free. Another traced a silken path over his sleeve, more joined it, formed a mesh which parted as he jerked his arm, lifted to settle on his hair. The smoke protected him, settled vapor preventing the silk from adhering as designed to do, maintaining the freedom of motion he needed. A rustle and his hand lifted, caught the hilt of the knife, slashed as mandibles snapped an inch from his cheek, slashed again to complete the ruin, then again to send the oozing creature from its perch to plummet below.

One taken care of—how many others would be waiting?

The things were the size of a small dog, legs doubling the body area, mandibles capable of closing around a neck. The hooked limbs could rip and tear flesh from bones, but the most dangerous part was the venom which would numb and paralyze with immediate effect. One bite, if it broke the skin, and he would be worse than dead.

A branch interrupted his upward progress and, in a sudden area of clarity in the smoke, he saw a scuttling shape, silk streaming from its spinnerets, limbs rasping as it lunged towards him. Chiton broke beneath the smash of his fist, covering his knuckles with ooze, and a thrust of his knife drove steel into the main ganglion, cutting and twisting and severing the muscles leading to the mandibles. Higher, and the smoke thinned, ebon wreaths tracing smears across the morning, soiling the first pearly light.

Touching the twinkle of diamond dew, which graced the clouds of gossamer hanging in delicate veils.

Laying a patina of darkness on the long shape shrouded and bound with layers of web to branches which crossed and made a platform.

A bier for the, as yet, undead.

Threnond was stung, paralyzed, locked in a mental torment of helpless awareness. Meat processed for later consumption by the newborn spiders which would hatch from the eggs festooning his chest and throat, his stomach, groin and thighs. Doomed to lie immobile while the hungry mandibles gnawed into his flesh. To know the horror of being eaten alive.

His eyes were open, glazed, already seats of torment. Targets for the glare of the rising sun. Blindness would be the first of his many extra hells.

There was no cure and only one mercy.

Dumarest administered it, then slid down the bole of the tree to land, coughing, doubled and retching as acrid vapor tore at his lungs. He heard Bochner cry a warning, then the impact of a sudden weight on his back, the snap of mandibles at his shoulders, the touch of chiton against his cheek. A touch which fell away as the hunter smashed the scrabbling spider to the loam, to thrust his wooden spear into its thorax, to crush it with his boot as it fretted the shaft.

Another which, crippled, moved slowly back up a tree. A third, which Egulus killed as Dumarest, fighting for breath, stumbled free of the smoke.

"So, you found him." Bochner glanced at the red smears where Dumarest had wiped his knife against his thigh. "And gave him an easy way out."

"Thank God for that." Egulus glanced uneasily up at the smoke. "I know what it's about now. Some spiders sting and paralyze, and others do not—how did you know which kind these are?"

"I didn't." Dumarest straightened, fighting a sudden giddiness. He had inhaled too much poison. "I just couldn't take the chance."

"He was lucky," said Bochner. "Threnond, I mean. He was damned lucky."

Dilys said, "Lucky? I thought he was dead."

"He is. That's what I mean." The hunter glanced at Dumarest. "Sometimes that's what a friend is for—and he had one of the best."

Chapter Eleven

The fire was small, the animal skinned and suspended over it slowly cooking, the smell tantalizing as it stimulated primitive appetites. Watching it, Dilys remembered her youth. Would the spit have been considered a machine? The means of starting the blaze? Vagrant thoughts, which grew in the dullness of fatigue. Fruits of an undisciplined mind.

Leaning back against a rock, she looked at the vast expanse of the sea far below. Light shimmered from the water in brief splinters of flashing brilliance, sparkles which caught the eye to vanish even as they were born, to flash again in a coruscating pattern of hypnotic attraction. A floor to match the sweeping bowl of the sky in which the sun hung like a watching, malefic eye.

And, suddenly, she was afraid.

All her life she had been confined. The village had been small and always there had been walls. Even later, when she had run away to the town to study, there had been close restraints; the cramped room she shared with others, the lecture halls, the classrooms, the workshops and, later, the interiors of ships, the engine rooms she had made her world. And now, agoraphobia gripped her so that she wanted to cringe and hide from the threat of the vast, open spaces.

"Dilys?" Dumarest was beside her. "Is anything wrong?"

Had she cried out in her sudden terror? Had he sensed her need? No matter, he was close and she felt a warm reassurance. Impulsively, she reached out to take his hand.

"Earl! Earl, I—"

"Should be watching the fire," he said quickly. "If you let the meat burn, I'll beat you."

He was joking, turning the subject from intense emotion,

and yet she sensed that it was not wholly a jest. If the need
arose he would beat her. Strike her, as he had killed
Threnond. From need. From mercy.

Could she have done the same?

Could Egulus?

They came from different worlds, she thought. To them,
the hull was the natural boundary, the hum of engines the
voice of the wind, the glow of lights the shine of the sun.
Planets were places to be visited and left without delay.
Worlds were names in an almanac. Here, on the dirt, they
were like stranded fish.

And she was tired. Tired!

They had dropped down the slope until clear of the
trees, then turned to the left where Dumarest had spotted a
long ridge running up the foothills. A relatively safe path a
few miles away, the distance trebled by the undulations of
the terrain, trebled again by the difficulty of progress. A time
of stumbling on, of drinking when they found water, eating
when they had food. Days which had passed into nights and
nights which had turned pale and become days again. How
many? She had forgotten.

"You're tired," said Dumarest, "but it won't be long now.
We're almost at the summit of the peak. Tomorrow we'll be
able to see what's on the other side." Then, when she made
no comment, he added, "Watch the meat, girl. Game is
scarce up here."

Game and fruits and even leaves succulent enough to
chew. He looked back down the slope as he left the girl,
frowning as he judged their progress. It was too slow. Hard-
ship had weakened them but here, facing the sea, was a bad
place to linger. Over the crest would be shelter and the possibility of larger game.

Egulus sat with the radio on his lap, Bochner beside him.
The captain was busy checking the mechanism, fingers deft as
he traced circuits and tested connections.

"It's crude, Earl." He looked up as Dumarest's shadow fell
over the mechanism. "Threnond had to use what was available, but he had limited knowledge of electronics. I'm trying
to alter the circuits a little to boost the emissions."

"It's still working?"

"Yes. I've tested the energy cell and it's viable. The thing
is, I'm not too sure of the emissions. It should be sending on

the general planetary band if it's to be any good at all, but there's no way of telling."

"Ships and field installations operate on a wide-band spectrum," said Dumarest. "They might not recognize it as a message at first, but they'll hear and investigate."

"By adjusting the receptors," agreed the captain. "If the operator on duty isn't a fool, or thinking of something else, or is willing to take the time and use the power. On any normal world I wouldn't be so anxious, but this is Hyrcanus."

"What difference does it make?" Bochner scowled. "There's a field, isn't there? A town of sorts? People!"

"Yes, but we have that, too." Egulus jerked his head at the sun. "And we're in the Quillian Sector. Space is full of noise. From here, you send word by courier and get it the same way. Close in, they can hear us but we don't know in which direction the field could be lying. It could even be on the other side of the planet."

"If it is?"

Egulus shrugged. "Luck," he said. "It's a matter of luck. They could pick up our transmission or it need never reach them."

And, even if it was heard, it could be ignored.

Dumarest said, "Can you increase the power? Send out an overall blast?"

"Maybe." The captain frowned, thinking. "If I can rig the circuits, yes. Threnond used the emergency alarm as a base and the capacitors are an integral part. He bypassed them, but they can be reincorporated. But if we do that, Earl, we'll be taking a chance. The power won't last."

"How long?"

Again the captain frowned. "I can't be sure. We've used up a lot during the journey. About three strong emissions, I'd say. Maybe one or two weak ones, then finish."

"A gamble," said Bochner. "If they don't hear us we'll have to make our own way." His teeth flashed in a smile as he thought about it. "Back to the beginnings, Earl. To hunt and trap and make do as best we can. It won't be too bad. We've skill and adaptability and we've a woman."

"Savages." Egulus looked at the radio. "I was on an expedition once. We'd heard about a ship which had been wrecked in the mountains of Glechen. We didn't find it but we found what could have been the survivors. They couldn't read, spoke in grunts, were covered in scabs and practiced cannibalism. Fifty years, maybe less, and they were back in the dirt."

"They were soft." Bochner echoed his contempt. "If a man is anything at all he'll find a way to make out, no matter what his environment. That's what life is all about, isn't it? To take what is and make it what you want it to be. Right, Earl?"

"Save the power." Dumarest ignored the question as he looked at Egulus. "Adjust the radio, but don't use it until we reach the summit." To the hunter, he said, "We'll eat and move on. You go ahead and scout. If you find anything of interest, just leave it. No private hunts. No risks."

Bochner said flatly, "Are you giving me orders?"

Dumarest caught the tone, saw the sudden tension, the stance which betrayed anger barely controlled. A reaction to fatigue too long denied, of nerves worn, yet masked by a casual facade. Of a maniacal pride which, even now, had to challenge the hint of another's authority.

He said mildly, "No, I'm not giving you orders. You stay with the others, if you want. I'll go ahead and scout."

"You think I'm tired?"

"I don't know what you are." Dumarest met the eyes, wild, wide, the irises edged with white. "But me, I'm bushed."

The admission brought the reaction he'd expected. Bochner relaxed, smiling, armored in his conviction of superiority.

"Hell, Earl," he said. "I'm bushed, too—a little. You go ahead and rest."

They reached the summit as darkness began to edge the horizon and the light of the dying sun threw streamers of red and gold, orange and amber against the vault of the sky. A spectacle which would have entranced Gale Andrel, but she, dead, had no eyes to see and they were too exhausted to do more than slump and stare at what lay beyond the peaks edging the shore.

A rolling savannah of bush and scrub, interspersed with clumps of trees now touched with the golden promise of the fading light. A stream which meandered toward a river which must wind on a slow and torturous path to the sea some distance to one side. Clouds, like smoke in the far distance, and beyond them, the soaring loom of mountains, their summits touched with perpetual white.

"Nothing!" Dily's voiced her disappointment. "Earl, there's nothing!"

Game trails, which his eye could see even in the dusk. Places which could conceal, timber which could make huts and fires, brush adaptable to protective stockades, and water which could be navigated, given craft which strong hands and sharp stones could build. A world in which men could live given the determination. But she saw nothing.

"No houses," she said dully. "No roads. No animals. No signs of life. A wilderness. It's a damned wilderness!"

"Easy." Dumarest caught her by the arm, his fingers relaying a warm comfort. "Just take it easy. Ask Bochner to start a fire and make some sort of a camp." It would give them both something to do. "Find some rocks and make sure they aren't harboring snakes. The night will bring wind, so bear that in mind. Come now!" He smiled and lifted up her chin. "Look on the bright side. There could be swamps or desert down there. Salt flats or marsh. Remember that place you spoke of on Swenna? Your land? Is it so different?"

"No," she admitted. "I guess not."

"Then why the disappointment? It should be like coming home."

But on Swenna there would be a town and neighbors, and even if they weren't close, they would be there and within contact range. Now she felt as if no one else but themselves existed on this entire planet. That they had crashed to live as best they might, to live and die without ever seeing the civilization she had known. The ships and towns and busy places. The markets and communes and the sound of eager voices.

Bochner said, "Gather fuel, woman. Get it while there is still light to see. And watch for snakes and things which could bite." His smile was ugly, that of a predator enjoying the moment before the kill. "Come now, move!"

The tone of command, which she had heard so often as a child and had never learned to like. For a moment she faced him, tempted to challenge his assumption that she would obey, to take him, hold him, use her hands to crush out his life. A moment only, then she recognized the weakness which made her less than the hunter. Sometimes, at rare intervals, she could overcome it, but always there had to be the stim-

ulus. Now it was easier to turn and move off to gather dried
grasses and broken twigs, patches of moss and windblown debris which would burn.

Egulus said, "Here, Earl? It's as high as we're going to get
unless we head for those mountains."

"Here." Dumarest looked at the sun, the sea bathed in
washes of color, swaths of warm and enticing hue which
matched and augmented the splendor of the sky. "But not
yet. Wait until its well after dark. We don't want to fight the
sun more than we have to."

"After dark," agreed the captain. "We've three good,
strong bursts, Earl. Shall I send them out quickly, one after
the other, or space them out?"

"Space them through the night. Send the last at dawn.
Wait, then use what power is left to do what you can."

"And if we get no response?" Egulus sucked at his lips as
Dumarest made no answer. "Maybe I can pick up something
by switching to reception. No luck so far, but the hills could
have blocked the signal. At least we might get a line as to the
whereabouts of the field."

And if not they could, perhaps, see ships coming in to
land. Others leaving—if they were on the right hemisphere.

Darkness brought a chill wind, which caught at the fire
and sent the flames dancing to paint the area in shifting patterns of light. From the shadowed savannah, something cried
out with a harsh, grating sound quickly ended. A beast falling
to the claws and fangs of a predator or the mating call of an
animal in heat. It was not repeated and Dumarest, standing
watch, guessed the former to be the most likely explanation.

He turned as Bochner came towards him. The hunter
looked at the cold gleam of the knife lifted towards him and
smiled.

"I could have killed you, Earl, had I wanted."

"Perhaps."

"You imply doubt. There is no doubt. I could have been
on you before you knew it. A move. A single blow and you
would be dead, now." The hunter drew in his breath, released
it with a soft inhalation. "My friend, I am a practical man
and know you are, also. What if rescue does not arrive?"

"We live."

"Of course, but how? I mean in what manner? Three men
and only one woman—you recognize the problem? The cap-

tain, I think, can be left out of the equation, but there is still you and me. Frankly, the need of a woman is, to me, only a minor irritation, but there is a question of principle. Of precedence. You understand?"

Dumarest remembered the cry he had heard—death sending its warning. Was he listening to another? Had he received it?

Against the glow of the fire the hunter's face was in shadow, the light which delineated his stance masking his expression, but there were things the shadows couldn't hide. The scent which came from him; the odor born of released adrenalin, of pulsing blood, of muscular tension and glandular secretions all designed to lift and hold the body to a fighting pitch. Odors Dumarest had smelled before when facing men in the arena. The stench which came through oil and sweat and which usually held the taint of fear. A taint now absent.

Bochner said again, "You understand?"

"Yes," said Dumarest, "I understand."

"And the woman?"

"Will make her own choice."

"I don't think so."

Dumarest looked at the shape limned in the firelight, the shadowed face in which reflected starlight betrayed the eyes. "I can't agree."

"So?"

"I think that as you're so wakeful you can take over the watch. Arguments can wait until later." He added dryly, "And don't worry, I won't creep up on you in the dark."

Dawn came with splinters of light and a wind which dropped as the day grew older. Dilys, refreshed by her sleep, tried to wash her face and hair in the dew which assuaged their thirst. Too little and too hard to collect, tantalizing rather than satisfying. When she complained, Dumarest waved at the savannah.

"We're too high for water up here. It's all running to lower levels."

"Why can't we wait down there?"

"Smoke." He looked at the fire. "Down lower it will be masked against the hills. Up here, it can be seen for miles."

The obvious, which she had overlooked. Irritably, she began to pile the remaining fuel on the embers.

"Save that until later," advised Dumarest, "until the morning winds have died. And if we're going to keep it fed, we'll need more fuel."

They descended to find it, dropping down the landward slope to gather and haul ferns and branches, twigs, roots, dried stems and saplings to be piled beside the fire. Dumarest downed a scurrying shape with his thrown knife and Bochner tried to emulate the feat. His blade pierced a leg and sent the rodent, screaming, to bite at the steel. Screams which died as he broke the creature's neck, but he was not pleased. Dumarest had killed clean at twice the distance.

"A dangerous man, that," said Egulus when, later, he watched with Dumarest beside the fire. Fed with the remaining scraps of available plastic, it threw an ebon column into the sky. "I saw his face when he realized you had bested him. He can't stand to be beaten at anything. I've known men like that before. I suppose, in a way, I was one myself. What I wanted, I had to get. I did, too—but that's over now. The *Entil* is gone."

"What do you know of him?"

"Leo Bochner?" The captain shrugged. "Nothing. He wanted passage and could pay for it. What else was there for me to know? You must have learned more about him than I did?"

A man who had boarded with expensive equipment; weapons and items of price, to be expected from a successful hunter and the representative of a wealthy consortium. His luggage was gone now, dumped with the rest of the jettisoned weight, and he had not protested. That, in itself, was unusual. In Dumarest's experience, the wealthy hated to lose their possessions; few were realistic enough to accept the necessity for sacrifice.

He said, "Anything on the radio?"

"Nothing." Egulus picked it up and tripped a switch. "I've been saving power. It's on to receive now. I—" He broke off, grunting with surprise. "I think—yes, by God! A signal!"

Dumarest listened to the sharp series of blips, the silence, the blips again.

As the following silence dragged he said, "Direction?"

"Hard to tell with precision." Egulus scowled at the instrument. "From land, though. Somewhere over there."

His hand pointed over the savannah, aimed above the

heads of Bochner and Dilys as they searched for edible grasses lower down the slope. Looking at her, the captain shook his head.

"Jumoke was a fool, Earl. He had no patience. I told him that your association with Dilys wouldn't last but he refused to listen. He even wanted to share. The bastard!" His hands tightened on the radio. "The crazy bastard! The work of a lifetime thrown away because he became obsessed with a woman!"

"It's over." Dumarest could appreciate the man's anger. "It's all in the past now, Captain."

"Yes." Egulus looked at his hands and eased their pressure. "Yes, Earl, but the woman is still with us. She still could be a source of trouble. You and Bochner—if she favors him, will you let her go?"

"I don't own her."

"Maybe she wishes you did. Maybe she'd want you to fight over her. You and Bochner like a couple of rutting dogs, with her watching and willing to mate with the one who wins." Egulus ended bitterly, "You and Bochner—I don't count."

Dumarest said quietly, "You're wrong, Varn. You and she have more in common than you think. You belong to the same world. Before Jumoke—were you close?"

"Yes."

"And she left you for the navigator?"

"She's her own master, Earl. You know how it is in space. We have our own customs and a captain has to respect them. And we were all partners, don't forget. Each of us technically equal to the other—hell, why waste time talking about it!"

"Check the radio," said Dumarest. "See if there are any further signals."

He added more fuel to the fire as the captain obeyed, damp leaves, mosses and green twigs which thickened the column of smoke into a brown-gray pillar against the sky. Turning, he stared toward the distant range of mountains. They were too far for him to make out other than general detail, but there could be mines and men working them and passes leading to farms beyond. Even a lone prospector, sending in a report, could have accounted for the signals.

An hour later they spotted the raft.

Chapter Twelve

Dilys watched as it came towards them, conscious of a tremendous relief. Soon, now, she would be on her way to houses and people. To the field and ships and the warm comfort and security of familiar things.

"They've come!" Her voice carried gladness. "They've come to rescue us!"

Egulus said, "They must have picked up our signals and come to investigate."

He was more cautious than the girl, and with reason. Investigation did not assume rescue; that implied payment and they had little to offer. A caution Dumarest shared.

"Spread out," he said. "Bochner, you take the left and I'll take the right. If they move against us, don't hesitate to act."

Orders which, for once, the hunter didn't object to obeying. He took up his position, looking at the advancing raft, head tilted, eyes narrowed.

"Small," he commented. "It could belong to a lone prospector or hunter."

"It's seen us," said Dilys. "It's heading directly toward the smoke."

Words spoken for reassurance—it had been obvious from the first that the raft was making for the peak on which they stood. Dumarest watched as it lowered its line of flight. Small, as Bochner had said, a hollow shell fitted with controls at one end, a rail around the body which would hold a padded seat. If there was a protective canopy, it was folded back. The body holding the antigrav units was equipped with landing skids, and the sound of the engine powering the units was a soft humming purr.

It would be holding one man at least, the driver. Then, as

148

he caught a blur of movement, Dumarest revised his figures. Two men, including the driver. The head he had seen toward the rear of the craft could not have belonged to the man at the controls.

"Two men." Bochner had also spotted the movement. "Either that's all there are or the rest are lying low. In which case, we could have a problem."

"Earl?" Dilys had heard and looked questioningly at Dumarest. "What does he mean?"

"Nothing. Just wave and call out."

To act the person in distress and to reveal the fact that she was a woman. Bait, if those who could be lurking inside the raft were scavengers; men who would kill for the sake of what they could steal. A good reason for landing if those within the vehicle were not the honest rescuers she thought.

The craft dropped lower, slowed, passed over them to swing in a wide circle over the sea before returning to settle gently on the edge of the summit.

Two men only, one at the controls, the other sitting in the body of the raft. A tall man, wearing dull fabrics and a peaked cap. One Bochner recognized. Caradoc, in disguise.

Oddly, he wasn't surprised.

The cyber glanced at him, then at the others. "Trouble?"

"Yes." Dumarest stepped toward the raft. "Our ship crashed and we're lucky to be alive. Can you take us to safety?"

"Of course." The smooth, even modulation held no hesitation. "Are there others besides yourselves?"

"No." Dumarest glanced at the man seated at the controls. Young, his face devoid of expression, hands resting on his knees. They were slim, with delicate fingers, the nails neatly rounded. He wore a loose robe of coarse brown material, the sleeves wide, the garment held by a cincture at the waist. "How did you know we were here? Did you pick up our signal?"

"Yes," said Caradoc.

"So we were lucky. A gamble which paid off." Dumarest added casually, "Did you have to travel far?"

"Twelve hours."

A thousand miles, at the usual touring speed of a raft and the rotation of Hyrcanus, was fast. They must have started out before the signal had been sent from the peak.

"A long time," said Dumarest. "It was good of you to take the trouble. Do you have any other business this way?"

"No."

"So you just picked up our signal and came straight to the rescue?" Dumarest glanced at the bundle within the raft. "Carrying survival gear, too, I see."

"An elementary precaution," said Caradoc. "Our action seems to disturb you. Why?"

Bochner could have told him and he stood, fuming, at the idiocy of the man. Even a young and inexperienced cyber should be aware that men did nothing without hope of reward. Certainly not the men living on worlds such as this. Fuel had to be paid for. The expense of the raft met. Time and energy expended in another's behalf had to be compensated for. At the very least, Caradoc should have asked what the party was prepared to pay for transportation. And Dumarest had been shrewd—that question as to the signal!

The answer had been as good as a confession.

"Disturb me?" Dumarest smiled and shook his head, lifting his hands as if to display their emptiness. Neither of the men in the raft were armed, as far as he could see. Another anomaly—but the wide sleeves of the robe the driver wore could cover more than wrists and arms. "Just the reverse. I am more pleased to see you than you can imagine. We are all pleased to see you. The alternative—" He broke off with a shrug. "Can you take us all aboard?"

"Unfortunately, that is not possible," said Caradoc. "The distance to be covered is long and we developed a fault which has lessened our load capacity. I can take one now, and make arrangements for the rest to be picked up later. You." He pointed at Dumarest. "I shall take you."

"No!" Bochner stepped forward, fighting to control his anger. The quarry was his and, he realized, now his only assurance of safety. Once the cyber had Dumarest, he would have no further use for the hunter. "Take me with you," he urged. "You can dump the survival gear, if you have to lighten the raft. Take me, too!"

A message made as plain as he dared if he hoped to maintain his pretense. And if Caradoc should betray him—what? To face Dumarest with naked blades? To attack and beat the cyber and his acolyte and, somehow, hold the quarry for later delivery?

Thoughts which spun and stilled as the cyber said, "That would be illogical. True, the possibility of an accident is small but, nevertheless, it exists. Without the survival gear we should be taking an unnecessary risk."

Dumarest said quickly, "Bochner! Hit them! Now!"

He was at the raft before the hunter had moved, reaching for the cyber, freezing as the driver whipped his hand into his sleeve and sent a beam of searing heat to pass a foot before his eyes. Another shot from the laser fused stone at Bochner's foot, a third sent smoke rising from crisped and incinerated hair.

"Yvan! Up!"

A touch and the raft had lifted, to hang poised in the air four feet from the edge of the summit and three above the uppermost level. From his vantage point Caradoc looked down at the group below.

Dumarest—the man the Cyclan had hunted for so long, now within his grasp. If Bochner had not spoken he would have been helpless now, drugged into unconsciousness by the hypogun clipped beneath the rail. And yet, would he have walked into the trap? Caradoc remembered the questions, the looks, the final command.

How had he known?

Bochner could have told him, but the hunter was at Dumarest's side, beating the last of the embers from his hair.

"They shot at us, Earl. Why, for God's sake?"

"The tall man's a cyber. The other is his acolyte. He didn't shoot to kill."

"I could argue that." Bochner touched his seared hair. "Are you sure that man's a cyber?"

"I'm sure." The tone, the lack of human curiosity, the failure to act as normal men would have acted. And the last, cold calculation which, coupled with his instinctive reaction, left no doubt.

"So, where does that leave us?" Bochner stared at the raft. A jump and he could reach it, but if the acolyte fired he would be dead when he did. And the man would fire, and had already shown his skill with the weapon now carried openly in his hand. "He could kill us, Earl. Burn us down."

All, but not Dumarest. He could be crippled, laser fire directed against his knees and elbows to leave him helpless. In-

juries which would leave his brain and the secret it held
intact.

Caradoc said, "A bargain, Dumarest. I guarantee the safety
of the rest if you will agree to accompany us."

A bargain from which he would gain nothing. Dumarest
looked at the raft, the acolyte standing at the controls, the
tall figure of the cyber at the rear of the vehicle. They were
too tense, too alert, for any plan he might make to have any
chance of success.

"I don't know you," he said. "Your name?" He nodded
when Caradoc gave it. "You are young but are obviously
clever. You should rise high and become a power in the Cyclan. My capture alone will assure that."

"You admit defeat?"

"Can I admit anything else?" Dumarest's shrug was visible
evidence of his acceptance of the situation. "But I'm curious
as to how you managed to trace me. It couldn't have been
easy."

"A matter of simple application."

"For you, perhaps, but far from simple to anyone else.
And after the *Entil* was wrecked? How could you have possibly known we would have reached this planet?" No cyber
could be flattered, but Dumarest knew of the single pleasure
they could experience, that of mental achievement. Caradoc
was young, and had already shown a certain carelessness. If
he could be persuaded to talk, to relax a little, and the
acolyte with him—it would be the only chance he would get.

He nodded as the cyber explained; the emergency signals
received, plotted, a line traced to Hyrcanus—work requiring
the application of a dedicated genius made ordinary in the
even modulation.

"And then, of course, you picked up our transmission."
Dumarest pursed his lips, a man obviously facing the inevi-
table, one willing to end a futile struggle. "Well, I guess that's
about it. If you'll bring the raft in closer, I'll jump aboard."

"No!" Bochner's voice was a snarl of anger. The knife he
lifted an edged splinter of brilliance as he lifted it to rest
against Dumarest's throat. "You take him then you take me,
or I'll kill him before your eyes!"

"Yvan!"

Dumarest spun as the acolyte lifted his laser, turning away
from the threatening steel, his hand dropping to his lifted

boot, his own blade rising, flashing as it lanced through the air, the winking brilliance of reflected light vanishing as the blade hit and plunged into living flesh.

As the acolyte fell, screaming, Dumarest sprang forward, throwing himself into the air as the raft lifted, the tall figure of the cyber falling, to hang half-suspended over the edge, blood welling from the charred hole burned in his side.

Dead or injured from the accidental shot, he was powerless to help or interfere. Dumarest caught at the rail, felt one hand slip, hung by the other as the vehicle rose into the air. Falling, the acolyte had hit the controls.

Dumarest glanced down, saw the land now far below, the faces of the others on the summit small blobs which shrank even as he looked. Wind from the sea caught his hair and chilled his face, pressing against his body with invisible hands, adding to the strain on his hand and arm. Heaving his body upward, he managed to send his free hand to grip the rail and hung, panting from the effort, his weakened body radiating messages of exhaustion. He wanted to rest, yet to wait too long was to invite disaster. Already his muscles ached from the strain of supporting his weight, the tissues of shoulders and arms a burning pain.

Waiting, he felt the raft tilt to the impact of the wind and heaved, one leg rising, foot and knee striving to reach and pass over the rail. An attempt which failed, and fresh pain flooded his arms and back as they took the strain of his falling weight. Sucking air into his lungs so as to hyperventilate his blood, he waited, then as the raft tilted, tried again. Blood roared in his ears and he felt the pounding of his heart as he heaved once more, the rail slowly coming closer to his chin, to pass beneath it, to press like a rod of heated iron against the soft flesh of his throat as he worked to get an elbow over the rail.

When he finally managed to flop into the open body of the raft, he was trembling and drenched with sweat. Able to do nothing but lie and breathe and wait for the strength to move. When finally he sat upright, the peak was a blur on the horizon, the plume of smoke from the fire a wavering thread against the sky.

The acolyte was dead, lying in a puddle of his own blood, one hand gripping the blade buried in his chest, sightless eyes staring at the sun. Dumarest recovered his knife and threw

the body over the side. As it fell, the raft lifted and he adjusted the controls, killing the lift and sending the vehicle back
towards the peak.

Incredibly, Caradoc was still alive.

He breathed in shallow gasps, small bubbles breaking at his
lips to form carmine circles, unconscious from shock and the
loss of blood. Dumarest lifted him from the rail and lay him
down beside the bundle in the body of the raft. The wound
was deep, the edges charred and blackened, but the very fury
of the blast had cauterized the flesh, staunching the wound
and sealing it against further loss of blood.

Dumarest looked at the hypogun where it rested against
the side just below the rail. He could guess what it contained.
Lifting it, he aimed at the cyber's flaccid throat and triggered
it twice. A double dose of drugs to send Caradoc into a
deeper oblivion.

"Earl!" Dilys came running as he grounded the raft.
"Thank God, you're safe! I saw something fall—I thought it
could be you!" She came to him, face wet with tears. "Oh,
Earl!"

Egulus said, "The way you moved! The speed! But what
happened? The cyber—"

"Is dead, I hope." Bochner thrust the captain to one side
and snarled as he saw the limp figure. "Kill him, Earl! Get
rid of the cold-blooded bastard!"

"Why?"

"He was after you, wasn't he? Chased you across space
from Ealius? Wanted to take you and hold you, right?"

"Right," said Dumarest. "But how did you know?"

"What? I—"

"Never mind." Dumarest stooped and lifted the limp body
of the cyber. "Here, take him. Set him down beside the fire.
You'd better cover him up with something. You could find
blankets in here." He lifted the survival kit and threw it after
the hunter.

Bochner looked at it. "Am I a nurse?"

"You're the fittest man here, aren't you? The best? You've
wanted to prove it often enough, so prove it now. You can
stay behind to look after the cyber. To take care of your
friend."

"You're mad." Bochner took a step toward where
Dumarest stood beside the raft. "Insane. What the hell do

you mean—my friend? Do you think I'm working with Cara-doc?"

"Are you?"

"No! And if you want to call me a liar, go ahead!" Boch-ner crouched, hands spread, an animal poised to spring. "Talk," he said. "It's just talk. You've no proof. I've been ex-pecting something like this. An excuse for you to turn against me. To take the woman for yourself. If the raft hadn't come, you'd have tried to put your knife in my back. Now you want to dump me. Leave me on this peak. Well, I've a better idea. You stay while I take the raft. You act as a nurse to the cyber while—"

He moved even as he spoke, the words serving as a distrac-tion, one which Dumarest had recognized. The hunter snarled, his hands slicing through empty air as Dumarest moved, anticipating the attack. Bochner turned, snatching at the knife he carried in his belt, grunting as Dumarest closed in, hand gripping his wrist, his own blade lifted to catch the sun.

For a long, dragging moment they stood, muscle set against muscle, bodies locked, poised in a composition which held the somber elements of death.

Too late, Bochner recognized the trap into which he had been lured. The weakness Dumarest had admitted, the fa-tigue, the earlier withdrawals from confrontation—all designed to deceive. Now he had met his match. Now he would die.

It waited in the glimmer of the blade, in the edge, the needle point, in the cold stare of the eyes so close to his own. In the bleak ferocity of those eyes which he had never seen before. In the strength against which he was helpless. In the determination which closed the space between the threatening point and his throat.

Closed it until no gap remained.

Pressed until the prick of metal bit into his skin.

"Go ahead," Bochner whispered. "Do it! Do it!"

Death, the supreme hunter, the thing which stalked a man all his life and, no matter how he should turn or twist, hide or run, was always victorious in the end. And what matter when the end came? Now, or in a year, made no difference. A dozen years, even, a score. What was a lifetime against eternity?

"Now," he breathed again. "Now!"

Strike and have done. To the victor, the spoils. To the winner, the loot and the fame and the glory. To the loser, only the restfulness of oblivion.

"No!" Dilys ran forward to catch at Dumarest's arm. "No, Earl! No! He saved your life!"

Once certainly, perhaps even twice. Dumarest felt again the cold rasp of chiton against his cheek and remembered how Threnond had died. Bochner had saved him then—and Caradoc needed a nurse.

"You bastard!" The hunter cried out in his rage as Dumarest shoved him back off balance. Recovering, he touched his throat and looked at the blood on his hand. "You cowardly bastard! You lack the guts to kill me!"

"The Cyclan will do that if you let him die." Dumarest gestured towards Caradoc. "You wanted a challenge? You've got one."

"To keep him alive up here while you take the raft? And then what? To carry him on my back over a thousand miles of wilderness?"

"I'll send back help."

"Maybe." Bochner looked at his hands. They were trembling. To be mocked, and before a woman. To be fooled. To be made to feel stupid—Dumarest should have killed while he had the chance. "All right, Earl. This round goes to you. But I won't forget. Damn you, I won't forget!"

Hyrcanus was small, the town named after the planet, the only town the world contained. The field was a patch of dirt seared and torn and dotted with discarded rubbish. The fence was a ring of scrub delineating the area, but there were ships waiting to leave and cargo needing to be loaded. From the window of his room in the tavern, Dumarest could see it all.

As could Dilys, at his side.

"That's the *Shalarius*," she said, pointing. "It's bound for Mucianus. And that's the *Zloth*. It's bound for Egremond."

"And that?"

"A private charter I think. Sealed hull, no contact, handler like a zombie."

Caradoc's vessel, and Dumarest wondered how long it would wait before sending out a rescue party. Not too long, he guessed, and it would be well to be far away when the cyber was found.

The woman seemed to be following his thoughts. "Did you mean it, Earl? About sending back help?"

"Yes."

"But you didn't specify just when." She frowned, thinking, trying to fill out gaps. "Why did you save him?"

"Bochner?"

"No. The cyber. You could have killed him. Thrown him after the acolyte. Why didn't you, Earl? He was after you, wasn't he? Chasing you, as Bochner said. Why leave him alive?"

Dumarest said, dryly, "A thousand miles, Dilys. A long way over unknown ground, and we weren't fit to begin with. How long do you think it would have taken?"

"Too long, if we could have made it at all. But what's that lot to do with it?" She blinked, understanding. "The raft. Caradoc brought us the raft."

"Yes."

"And saved us from having to walk. Perhaps he even saved our lives. And you spared his because of that?"

Because of that, and because the man had been hurt, helpless and dying, perhaps already dead if Bochner had failed to administer aid, or the wound had proved beyond treatment.

"You're a strange man, Earl." Dilys reached out to touch his hair, her fingers traveling down over his cheek to linger on his lips. "So hard and strong, at times, and so gentle at others. I think I sensed it from the first. It was something I needed. Something I shall always need. Earl—must it end?"

She read the answer in his eyes.

"Yes, I suppose it must, something else I've known from the beginning. But it hurts. Poor Jumoke—how it hurts!"

But not for long, and not as badly as she chose to think, at the moment. A quick, clean cut, with a minimum of pain, leaving a wound which quickly healed. She would not be left alone.

Dumarest turned from the window as Egulus entered the room. "And luck?"

"Some." The captain sat down, lifted the bottle standing on the table and poured himself a glass of wine. Lifting it, he looked at the murky amber of the local produce and said,

"The *Shalarius* can give us all passage if we can pay. High only, no Low—the journey is too short for that. On Mucianus, I've word of a friend who has a ship undergoing repair. I think he could use an ex-captain."

"And an engineer?"

"I guess so." Egulus looked at the woman then at Dumarest. "But I thought—"

"I belong with you, Varn. We share the same world." Her hand fell to his shoulder to squeeze with a warm intimacy which squared his shoulders and took years from his face. "We'll get along."

"Without money?"

"We have money." Dumarest reached into his pocket and spread the table with sparkling glitters. The stones he had taken from Threnond's belt which the man had used as a repository for his wealth. "These can be sold to gain enough for our passages."

"Ours?" Egulus looked the question. "Are you coming with us?"

Dumarest shook his head. "No. I'll make my own way."

"On the *Zloth?* It's heading back into the Rift."

Back into the region where suns were close and space was a maze of conflicting energies. Where a ship could hide and a man get lost. To where once again he could take up his search for Earth.

The End.

BESTSELLERS FROM ARROW

All these books are available from your bookshop or newsagent or you can order them direct. Just tick the titles you want and complete the form below.

PROMISES	Charlotte Vale Allen	£1.95
THE AFTER DINNER GAME	Malcolm Bradbury	£1.75
THE KGB DIRECTIVE	Richard Cox	£1.75
MCENROE	Tania Cross	£1.50
GOD BLESS THE BORDERS!	Lavinia Derwent	£1.25
WELLIES FROM THE QUEEN	Colin Douglas	£1.50
A DISTANT SUNSET	Virginia Ironside	£1.50
ONE STEP AT A TIME	Marie Joseph	£1.50
PAINTED BIRD	Jerzy Kosinski	£1.60
SCANDALS	Barney Leason	£1.95
THE CHAMDO RAID	John Miller	£1.60
PIN	Andrew Neiderman	£1.50
WHITENIGHTS, RED DAWN	Frederick Nolan	£1.95
TORPEDO RUN	Douglas Reeman	£1.50
WOLF TO THE SLAUGHTER	Ruth Rendell	£1.50
THE EXPERIMENT	Richard Setlowe	£1.75
SONGS FROM THE STARS	Norman Spinrad	£1.75
MORE TALES FROM A LONG ROOM	Peter Tinniswood	£1.50
THE FACTS OF RAPE	Barbara Toner	£1.75
THE CLAW OF THE CONCILIATOR	Gene Wolfe	£1.60
	Postage	
	Total	

ARROW BOOKS, BOOKSERVICE BY POST, PO BOX 29, DOUGLAS, ISLE OF MAN, BRITISH ISLES

Please enclose a cheque or postal order made out to Arrow Books Limited for the amount due including 10p per book for postage and packing for orders within the UK and 12p for overseas orders.

Please print clearly

NAME ....

ADDRESS ....

....

Whilst every effort is made to keep prices down and to keep popular books in print, Arrow Books cannot guarantee that prices will be the same as those advertised here or that the books will be available.